For Tamara

JENNIFER GRIFFITH

ISBN: 9781706223894

Cover art by Blue Water Books, 2019. Stock photo credit © Mika @ AdobeStock.

Chapter 1

Bing

Bing Whitmore stomped toward the stables, the gravel crunching beneath his work boots. "It's not about the loss of income, Freya."

Yes, he should have developed thicker skin for this business by now, but when Rose Red's leg broke, it nearly broke Bing in the same type of complex fracture.

Splintered him.

Yes, horse breeding and racing were risky ventures, and getting too attached to individual horses increased the risk exponentially, but the problem was, Rose Red's fracture followed hot on the heels of losing million-dollar Torrey Stakes winner Snow White just that summer.

"You love the horses." Freya double-stepped to catch up with him. "More than anything or anyone. I get that, Bing." She brushed the collecting snowflakes off her shoulders. "We all do. It's in our Whitmore blood."

"Then you get why I need to quit." Quit horses. Quit all of it.

"Quit! Owners don't quit."

"They do if they sell their shares of the business to the other partners."

"But, Bing!" Freya gasped. "You're the one who runs the day-to-day aspects of Whitmore Stables. The rest of us are owners because of

Grandpa, but we're not exactly involved, not like you are."

"Well, then you can hire someone to replace me. A professional." Someone who wouldn't go Three-Mile Island every time he picked up a curry comb to clean off a dusty flank or smelled leather. "Lots of guys out there would kill for a chance to manage a stable full of thoroughbreds."

"Bing." Freya slid her glasses off her head and balanced them on the end of her nose. "What's really going on here?"

Uh-oh. It never worked in his favor when Freya started using her PhD in psychology on him. "I don't need any head-shrinking, not even with the family discount."

"Is this about the surgery? Rose Red is getting better."

She'd never race again. Although—at least she was alive. If that rookie veterinarian hadn't shown up, Bing would have lost Rose Red, too.

And then what? Bing would have wandered off into the snow-covered hills with just the clothes on his back and become a statistic.

"Fine. No head-shrinking. And I can see you're not going to answer any of my probing, empathetic questions—so I'll just give you some unsolicited advice."

Which he would reject, obviously.

"Don't quit. Or sell. Or whatever. Not today."

Maybe tonight, then. "It's what's best for Whitmore Stables, Frey."

"What about a vacation?"

"People in my line don't take vacations." Animal care wasn't the kind of thing that could just be put on hold. The horses needed food, exercise, and close supervision. "In my eight years at Whitmore, I haven't missed a day."

"That's what I'm talking about." Freya punched his upper arm. "You need a break. Maybe some easygoing socialization with humans instead of animals. You've been through a lot this summer and fall. That'd be rough on anyone."

2

No kidding. He crossed his arms over his chest. And he wasn't getting into dating, if that was what Freya was hinting with her *easygoing socialization* verbiage.

They stood at the door of the stables, the wind howling and the snow collecting.

"Fine. Say you did quit, walk away from this—that would be a permanent vacation. You might not like it. Did you think of that? How about just giving it a trial run first? Just like you'd do with the horses, practice runs before a race."

Bing shut his eyes. Freya would gloat if he agreed she was making sense.

"Honestly, I wouldn't even know how to take a vacation. I need something long term."

"Look, I'll talk to Dr. Harrison, see if he has someone he can recommend to man the stables for a few days"—she startled when she must have seen his face—"make that *weeks*. Then, I'll look around online for a good vacation spot and book you something completely quiet. A hotel with nobody else even staying in it. Maybe in the mountains somewhere like Steamboat Junction or Wilder River. You used to ski when we were kids. Remember?"

This wouldn't work. Going away wouldn't make him want to come back. However, being in the mountains might give him some peace. "I totally beat you down that black diamond run."

"Ha! That was the beginners' hill and you know it."

"But the story is better my way."

"So you'll do it? I'm a great sleuth when it comes to finding off-the-beaten-path vacation spots. Not that I ever go to them, but this will be my big chance."

"You're going, too?" A little company might not hurt. "Uh, okay."

Freya pulled off her glasses. "You'll do it? I can make the plans?"

"Like you said, a trial run." But his gut said he was through with horses forever.

Chapter 2

Ellery

The numbers on the ancient ledger blurred. Ellery Hart blinked to get them to come back into focus. They couldn't be right, could they? She gripped the counter of the hotel's front desk and willed the number on the negative side to be mistaken—and to float over to the positive side of the ledger.

It didn't.

Which meant one thing: the Bells Chalet was in trouble.

"Hey, cutes!" Kit slid up to Ellery and bumped her hip, a sprig of holly glued to the headband in her voluminous yellow hair. "We got a booking through that clearinghouse site online. It's for the suite."

"A booking?" They'd need more than *a* booking to erase this big, scary number in the red column. "That's great. Thanks for setting up our account with them. You're getting really good at the marketing stuff."

"Uh, not really. You don't have to fib. But hey, what I'm here to tell you is that they're arriving today. Soon! Should I get Lenny to shovel the walk?"

Had it snowed again enough to cover the steps? Already? This winter's snow should have brought scads of guests to the Bells Chalet. The ski slopes were teeming with out-of-towners. So *why* wasn't Ellery's hotel teeming as well?

"Sure. Shoveling the walk is a good idea. We don't want anyone to slip and fall." Especially since Ellery might be behind in her liability insurance payments, along with all her other payments. "Are they an older couple?"

"Bing and Freya Whitmore from Massey Falls is all I know." Kit shrugged.

Massey Falls was south of the border, not a short trip. They'd be tired. Ellery wished the mattresses in the suite were better and guaranteed a restful night's sleep. Not that she could afford to upgrade them now.

"Their names do sound old. I'll track down Lenny." The back door banged and Kit hollered, "Lenny, my boy! Where are ya?"

Maybe Ellery needed to hold a staff meeting on professionalism. Not that any guests were around to hear Kit's bellowing.

A commotion outside the front door blasted through the reception area like a winter storm. Ellery practically jumped over the desk as she ran to see what caused the clatter and yelps. "Are you all right?" Ellery hustled out into the chilly afternoon air on the porch. "Oh, my goodness, let me help you with this."

A man and a woman and five suitcases created a jumble at the bottom of the icy front steps beside a shiny black truck. The man crouched down, and the woman patted his shoulder. "I'm so sorry, Bing. Is your ankle okay? I can take you to urgent care. There's probably one nearby."

Holy crud—the guy was hurt! Dang it! The one day Ellery hadn't made Lenny clear the walkway and steps of snow and ice.

"I have some medical training." Ellery might only have her CNA license, but a certified nurse's assistant was better than nothing in an emergency. "Can I take a look?"

The woman helped Ellery pile the suitcases out of the way. This was a lot of suitcases. How long had these people been planning to stay? A month?

Well, not a chance of that anymore.

Worse, Ellery was going to get sued. Just when she'd thought things couldn't get worse!

Finally, Ellery came around and knelt in front of the guy—and caught sight of him. *Kablam!*—what a looker. Dang, with that thick head of dark hair and those soulful brown eyes, she was gazing at the best-looking man to ever set foot in Wilder River.

Of course, he was with his wife, so Ellery shouldn't even be noticing his looks. Or his scent. Something like leather, earthy and strong.

Dang it. It had to stop now. She'd never been this unprofessional toward a guest in all her years working at Grandpa's hotel.

"Should we pull off your boot so I can take a look?" Ellery reached for the heel of the well-worn work-boot. This footwear wasn't for show, like that of so many of the fancied-up tourists who usually came to Wilder River.

"It's fine," he said. "It's nothing." He looked up and met Ellery's gaze, locking it there for a moment too long.

"It's *not* nothing, Bing," his wife said, cutting off the source of the buzzing electricity inside Ellery at last. "Let the cute nurse look at it."

Cute nurse? Ellery's glance darted at the wife, who had a severe haircut, cat-eye glasses, and the same dark hair and eyes as her husband's. They say opposites attract. However, sometimes like draws like—and this couple exemplified it. Weird that the woman would compliment Ellery to her husband, though. That was strange, right? Did wives do that?

Only those very secure in their relationships, most likely.

"At least let her check whether your leg is broken."

His eyes flashed up at his wife. "It's *not* broken," he nearly growled.

Wow, he could be intense.

He exhaled, closed his eyes and shook his head. "Sorry." He turned to Ellery and opened his dark eyes. "I just don't like talking about broken bones. It's a thing with me."

6

Noted. "I'm sure you know best." The customer always did. She backed up, bumping against the huge truck.

"Fine." The wife huffed. "If it's not broken, then get up and carry our suitcases up the steps."

"Oh, no-no-no." Ellery popped to her feet. "I'll have our porter do that." Lenny could be termed a porter, right? Handyman, gardener, porter, etcetera.

Lenny appeared at the top of the steps with a snow shovel. "I gots the salt, too, Ellery." He grinned wide as the Wilder River itself, making the crow's feet at the edges of his eyes more pronounced. "The salt melts the ice, Pops always said."

Pops. Lenny still called Grandpa Bell *Pops*, though he'd been gone five years.

"Thanks, Lenny. But could you help our guests with their luggage instead?" She stood up and indicated the pile of suitcases. "They'll be in the suite on the top floor."

"Nice!" Lenny grinned again. "That's the room with the best view. You'll like it a lot." He bounded down the stairs, squeezed Ellery around her shoulders, and collected all five suitcases at once, the lovable hulk. "Won't they, Ellery?"

"I hope so, Lenny."

"Is you hurt, mister?" Lenny paused, looking down at the guest. Then, balancing everything, he reached a hand down and lifted the guy to his feet. "It's cold out here. Come inside. There's a hot tub in your room. You and the missus should warm up."

The two guests exchanged horrified glances. What—they didn't like hot tubs? They were worried that it wouldn't be clean? If nothing else, Ellery kept the rooms sanitized.

"Oh, we're not—" Mrs. Whitmore said.

Ellery didn't want to hear about their fears about cleanliness. "The jets in the hot tub get great reviews." She bustled to hand a small piece of luggage to Lenny, who tore up the steps. "Now, if you're sure you're okay to walk, let's get you checked in."

He was sure, and they started climbing. As they approached the top of the stairs, Ellery stole a glance at Mr. Whitmore's reflection in the glass. Why were all the best ones taken?

"You work here?" At the top of the steps, he held the door for her. "I thought you were some kind of angel or good Samaritan sent to help men tripped by too much luggage before they even start climbing the stairs to the hotel."

Ah, so maybe no one had fallen down icy steps after all. Hallelujah. It was a Christmas miracle. "I own the Bells Chalet."

"Isn't that nice?" the wife said, winking at her husband. "So, I take it that means we will be seeing a lot of you while we're here?"

"Only as much of me as you'd like."

"Oh, I think we'll want to see quite a bit of you, Mrs.—?"

"Ellery Hart." *Miss* Ellery Hart. Sure, she'd almost been a Mrs. once. Not that the *almost* mattered now. "Pleased to have you at our hotel. I hope you'll find it a quiet retreat."

"That's exactly what Bing needs." The wife cuffed his chin with a curled fist.

"Thanks, Freya." He smirked.

Ellery led them into the lobby, shooting a silent prayer upward that this nice—if slightly strange—couple wouldn't notice the emptiness or the run-down nature of the chalet and immediately check out.

***

"Who was that couple?" Mom fluttered up to Ellery's side as soon as the Whitmores disappeared up the stairs. "So stylish! And he's like that one movie star from that detective show I used to watch all the time. Dreamy. You should get to know him."

"Mom. I'm not in the habit of flirting with married men."

"Fine." Mom harrumphed. "So ethical. Who taught you to be that way?" She swiped one of the red and white mints from the bowl and crinkled the cellophane.

"You did." Ellery pinched Mom's cheek. "Now, listen. We have to do everything we can to make sure they enjoy their stay. They already had a bumpy start."

"I heard about the guy's leg. It didn't look broken to me. It looked *fine*." She held out the *i* in fine.

"Mom!"

Mom huffed. "Ellery, I'm only prompting you because I wish you'd quit shutting your eyes to handsome men. Notice someone, already."

Oh, Ellery had noticed. Her spine still tingled from the effect of his gaze. "What I noticed was his wife, Mom."

"Oh, bosh. He wasn't married to her. Zero chemistry between them. Speaking of noticing, sniffing out chemistry is my specialty."

Oh, was it now? Eye-rolling could be Ellery's specialty in that moment. "Let's move on."

But Mom couldn't. "If you're not going to flirt with the guests, then at least rip the blindfold off and realize that Allard Allman is buzzing around you like a fly to honey."

It was bees to honey. "The banker? He just wants to be paid, not date me." The loan Ellery had taken out eighteen months ago to keep the hotel afloat in the expectation that Bells Chalet's business would pick up once the ski season rolled around, had a balloon payment coming due. Not good news for the Big Red Number in her ledger.

"I wouldn't put money on that bet, if I were you."

"Frankly, Mom, I couldn't put money on anything at this point."

Kit appeared. "Money troubles?" Her fingers did a spider-crawl across the desk toward the ledger again. "You'll think of something."

Mom tossed her high ponytail. "Have you considered the idea that if you were to date and marry Allard Allman, your assets would combine and the loan payment would *poof!* disappear?"

"Mom!" How unethical would that be? Far worse than noticing a guest's fathomless dark eyes and legend-inspiring dark hair. "I'm not interested in Allard Allman. Ice that whole idea."

"You're the icy one."

Lenny lumbered down the steps from the guests rooms. "You gots money problems, Ellery? I can help. I've been saving my change from eating at YooHoo Chicken for about, oh"—he looked at the rafters—"seventeen years. It's all the way to the top of my Rudolph jug now. You could have it, if you need it."

Lenny's earnestness thawed Ellery's glacier heart. "That's so generous, Lenny. But you don't have to do that. Things will work out."

"But you could. Just so you know." Lenny was sweeter than candied pecans. "If I gots it, it's yours."

"You're the best man in this whole town, Len." Ellery squeezed his arm.

Kit slid the ledger off the counter and flipped it shut. "I'm sure you'll think of something, Ellery. And we'll all support you."

Mom chuckled slyly. "Especially if it involves marrying a rich man."

"Truvie!" Kit said. At least someone was coming to Ellery's defense. "Ellery is going to marry for love."

"She tried that once. Didn't work out. Now, she should know better."

Mom was hopelessly gauche. Too bad the truths didn't bounce off Ellery as easily as they should have.

"Everyone! Back to work." Ellery took the ledger and its terrible truth from Kit's grasp. "We're going to make these guests' stay the best they've ever experienced. And I'm going to come up with an idea to save the chalet."

Mom beamed.

Ellery threw a shroud on that beam. "An idea that does *not* involve exploiting a man for his bank account." She pounded a fist on the counter, and the decorative pile of sleigh bells Kit had set out for charm jingled.

Were they the merry bells of hope, or the death knell of the Bells Chalet? *Bong, bong, bong.*

Chapter 3

Bing

"**B**ingham Whitmore! Wake up!" Freya flopped down on the bed beside him, jostling his shoulder and making his ankle sting. "You're on vacation. Don't sleep it away."

Wasn't that the point of vacations?

"We've been in this room for twenty minutes, after a nine-hour drive. You weren't the one at the wheel. You were doing your nails. Since when do psychologists pay that much attention to their fingernails?"

"You got something against manicures?"

"No, but why put on paint just so it can chip off?" What a waste of time. That woman downstairs, Ellery Hart or whatever, had had clean hands, tidily trimmed nails, and no glitter bombs or teensy jewels on them. Not that he'd been noticing her. Much. "Hands are our most important tools. Nobody decorates a hammer."

"Whatever. When did you turn into such a curmudgeon? You used to be ..."

What? What did he used to be? Before everything fell apart? "Almost as charming as I am now?"

"Charming! Shah! The way you rip-snorted at the gorgeous owner of the hotel? You'd call that charm?"

He had snorted, hadn't he? "I did apologize."

Freya rolled off the end of the bed and plopped into the recliner beside the fire. She extended the foot rest and leaned back. "This room has charm, even if you don't." She patted the armrest. "I love the fireplace. And if I ever get married, I'm totally going on a honeymoon somewhere with a hot tub." She waved a hand toward the Jacuzzi in the corner. "I booked it because the reviews said it was a quiet ghost town. I wonder why no one else seems to be staying here."

True, the parking lot downstairs had been eerily empty. "Quirky staff?"

"That big lug who lugged my luggage had a heart of gold. He even refused to take my tip. He only took loose change, he said. Bless him."

The guy hadn't seemed all there to Bing. "I'm just grateful for the quiet. Now, let me doze off, Frey."

"Fine—but for no more than an hour. We're checking out the nightlife in this town. I may be a girl-cousin-person, but this evening I'm your wing-man, and you're finding someone to have a fling with while you're here."

A fling! "That's not happening." Not a chance in Santa's workshop, which was what the front of this hotel looked like.

"Oh, come on, Bing. There's abso-bloomin'-lutely no one for either of us to date in Massey Falls, and you know it. Love the hometown or not."

"As if Wilder River is any bigger." He pulled off his boots. Ouch. That ankle was an alarming size. Perfect start of a vacation, looking like a complete klutz in front of that pretty woman. Oh, and then snarling in front of her. For the win.

"Wilder River is obviously bigger. More eclectic. It's got ten times as many people, and much, *much* cuter hotel proprietresses."

Please. As if she'd even look at him after what he'd done. Besides, that girl downstairs was way too gorgeous to not be involved with someone. To confirm the fact, she hadn't sloughed off the *Mrs.* when

Freya had thrown it at her. "She's married."

"The way she looked at you? I doubt it."

How had she looked at him? "What I need is some R-and-R. Not a fling."

"Can't rest and relaxation include a fling?"

"I wish you'd stop using that word."

"You used it too, Bing. Bing-Bing. Bing-needs-a-fling."

If she didn't knock it off right now—"I'm coming off a troubled relationship, in case you haven't noticed."

"What! You—you were dating that female jockey? I never heard. Shayla … Shayla … what was her last name?"

Some people! "Do you even take an interest in the racing world, Freya? Her name is Shayla Sharp. Everyone who knows anything about racing knows the name of the sole female jockey in the history of the sport to take home a victory at the Torrey Stakes."

Freya huffed loudly. "Forgive me! I'm still just in shock that you were in a relationship with her."

But he wasn't. "We went on one date."

"And that's what you deem *coming off a troubled relationship?*" The scoffing filled the whole room, carpet to rafters. "Bing. You know how lame that sounds, right?"

"Don't use the term lame." Lame horses were a sticking point. "Just don't."

Slowly, Freya nodded. "Oh, I get what you're saying now." Her face went from joking to grim. "Are they really going ahead with the burial outside the Torrey Stakes racetrack? That's such an honor for Snow White."

One normally reserved for the likes of Secretariat. "Yes, and the bronze statue of her." The organizers' mourning had mirrored everyone's at Whitmore Stables. "Her death came so soon on the heels of her victory there, the whole community was in shock."

And Bing was still suffering the effects of that shock. Electrocution, wasn't that what it was called? That heart-stopping death?

Since that day, he hadn't been able to detect his own heartbeat, other than during the terrible squeezing pressure of pain when he'd thought he was losing Rose Red, too.

"Hey." Freya's voice was softer now. Less chiding. "Dude. Do you really think it's healthy to replace human relationships with horse relationships? Snow White and Rose Red are beautiful creatures, but they're no substitute for what you really need."

And now his cousin was asserting herself as the expert on what Bing *really needed.* "You sound more like a meddling aunt than a trained psychological professional right now. Just warning you."

Freya set the chair aright and pulled her glasses down onto her nose. "Tell me about your relationship with Rose Red."

"They'll ride you out of Hamburg on a rail for that terrible German accent."

"Fine. Let's just figure out how to get you to snap out of whatever this funk is. Me, I think a beautiful woman could be a funk-snapper. Forgive me for presuming to notice that you're a lonesome bachelor bumping along towards the age of thirty with nothing and nobody to show for it."

"You really should be a professional. You're totally good at this empathy and therapy thing." Bing had had enough of this. He slid off the bed and headed for the bathroom. Chances were, Freya wouldn't harangue him through the door. Maybe. "I'm feeling worlds better already."

"Stop it. Fine. I'll ask you a question from my training then. When was the last time you rode a horse? Or worked with one directly?"

Bing stopped in his tracks so fast, the soles of his feet could have had carpet burn. "I'm going to soak my ankle in ice water."

"You can't avoid your problems and your feelings forever. You have to face them."

"I happen to know you're referencing the head nun on *Sound of Music* right now."

"Mother Superior."

Right. Whatever.

"And for the record, the fact that you have watched *The Sound of Music* often enough to recognize quotes from it makes you an even *more* eligible bachelor." Freya didn't care that he'd closed the bathroom door and was running the cold water in the tub. "Women don't just want money and good looks, you know. They want conversation. About topics that interest them—topics like movies, if they're any fun at all."

"Don't forget charm. They want charm."

"Bummer for you." Freya paused. Maybe she'd gone away. Nope. "Just kidding. I was waiting for you to laugh."

He should send her outside to fetch some snow to throw in this water for the ice-water effect on his swelling.

"Come on, Bing. That's what you used to be—a laugher. Let's get that back—fling or no fling—on this trip."

With or without laughter, what Bing *really* needed—add some air quotes for Freya's sake—was a detectable heartbeat again.

"Hey, hurry up in there. I'm dying for some dinner. Let's walk up to the town."

Chapter 4

Ellery

"If we don't have any more bookings coming in, I think I'll walk up town." Ellery handed the key to the cash drawer to Kit. "For inspiration."

"Do you like my decorations? What I've done so far?" Kit pocketed the key. "It livens up the place a little, eh?"

Not enough. For the first time in a while, Ellery eyed the lobby with a critical eye. Even though the way Grandpa had laid it out forty years ago felt sacred, maybe it was time to refresh. Just because Ellery and Mom and Lenny and Kit looked at the reception area and saw Grandpa Bell's devotion to the hotel, that didn't mean guests had the time-travel-to-nostalgia vision they did.

Ellery squeezed her eyes shut, mentally donned a fake identity of someone who'd never set foot in here while the ebullient Grandpa— Pops—Bell owned the place, and then opened her eyes and looked around.

Nope. It was a big, old nope.

The Bells Chalet sat squarely in the time vacuum between current and vintage—in the black hole known as *dated*. Pink and mint green tiles stretched across the front of the honey-oak desk. That look complemented the desert-scene printed curtains—with cactus and little step-pyramid diamonds—in pastel purples and teal. And the furniture looked like it had been salvaged from behind a thrift store, where it had been dumped because no one bought it.

Not to mention the dark-purple painted walls.

Nope. It was a *big* old nope.

"Where are you, Ellery? La-la land?" Kit walked up with a pile of fresh towels. "I can do some Pinterest searches if you don't like what I've done to make it feel like the holidays in here. But, uh, unless you want me to raid my mom's ridiculously hoarder-level fabric stash to make bows and things, I'd need a budget."

That was just it. There was no budget. Not even for the loan payment. "What you've done is great, Kit. I'll be back in a while."

The door jingled behind her as Ellery left. Outside, she sucked in a sharp breath of icy air. She tugged her crocheted scarf closer to her neck. This year was going to be a cold one. Might even be too cold for the ski crowd soon.

With the slopes open for the past six weeks, surely Bells Chalet should have had some bookings. Yeah, she had an ugly foyer, and the whole place needed a refresher, now that she was ready to admit the truth—but at her prices, she should have *some* guests. A new chain hotel was going up down the street, and so the market should be ripe for it, right?

The spot in her brain right behind the bridge of her nose hurt. She marched up the street toward the main area of shops and cafés, every footstep pounding harder into the crunch of crusted snow. Her hotel's location was good—within walking distance of town. What was she lacking?

A husband, her mother would say. Cue Ellery's eye-roll again. Mom could even make her into a disgusted teenager in absentia.

"I don't need a husband!" she said, each syllable matching a stomp.

Naturally, laughter broke out nearby, where a couple of—yup—teenage girls were staring at her from their perches at bistro tables outside the espresso shop. What kind of idiots sat outside to drink

17

coffee in these temperatures? Ellery winced and gave a fingers-only wave. The girls just laughed more.

Nice.

First she'd flirted with a married man, and now she was humiliating herself in public. Maybe she shouldn't have come downtown. Maybe she should have just gone to her room and done internet research. *How do I save a dying hotel?* Surely there were thousands of articles with great ideas just waiting to save her livelihood and Grandpa Bell's legacy.

"Why, if it isn't Miss Ellery Hart." Allard Allman stepped directly into Ellery's path, stopping her determined march toward ... what? Toward nothing. "Nice weather we're having."

"It is if you want to go around in your drawers all day," she mumbled. Why did quotes from the crusty Mayor George Shinn of *The Music Man* and other non sequitur musical quotes have to erupt at the worst times? Like when she was confronted by the man who held her—and her employees'—future in his hands?

"What was that?" Allard Allman took off his beret. "I didn't hear you." But he didn't wait for her to restate. Bless him. "I mean it's nice weather we're having *if* we want the ski tourism business to boom, of course."

"Right." Of course. "Tourism is so important to our town's economy."

"Speaking of economy, your hotel's finances are doing well, I take it."

He knew darn well they weren't well. "Of course. Of course! We've got happy guests today, for sure."

Probably. If they didn't need to spend the bulk of their vacations in urgent care instead of on the ski slopes.

"Good. Glad to hear it." Allard Allman took a step closer.

Without the hat, he stood an inch or two shorter than Ellery. Not that she was a towering giantess, but she was wearing heeled boots today. Anyway, the closeness of their height meant his breath blew

18

straight into her face. She knew because in this good-for-tourism weather, it was steamy-visible.

And it smelled like Swiss cheese.

"I'll see you later, Mr. Allman."

"Call me Allard, please, Ellery."

She hadn't exactly given him permission to address her by her first name. It rankled. She just nodded and scooted around him.

"If you're not too busy taking care of those guests and keeping them happy, I'd like to pop by the Bells Chalet and discuss non-business topics some evening soon. Maybe tomorrow night, say, around seven?"

A pair of tall figures strolled up beside Ellery, flanking her. The Whitmores! "Oh, hello." They'd passed the banker and possibly heard her exchange with him.

They didn't address her, but instead, the wife spoke to Allard Allman. "I'm afraid Ms. Hart will be far too busy at the hotel."

Yup, they'd heard the conversation.

"We're her executive suite guests, see? And we are going to require far too much personal attention for her to break away. I'm so sorry."

Ellery could have hugged the woman. "The customer is always right." She tilted her head limply at Allard Allman, whose eyes tightened at the sides.

"Naturally." He huffed and turned to go back into the bank. "Good day, Miss Hart."

When Allard Allman disappeared, Ellery gave Mrs. Whitmore a sheepish smile. "How could you tell I needed an extraction?"

"From the rabbit-in-a-spotlight look in your eyes, maybe?" Mr. Whitmore looked even handsomer in the pink light of the fading day. "Or maybe it was the way your leg was poised to kick him in the neck if he got any closer."

In his double-breasted pea coat, with the collar turned up, Bing Whitmore looked practically dashing. Blast him! And why was he so funny? He didn't laugh at his own jokes, but neither could Ellery. She couldn't flirt with a married guy. Laughing was flirting, right? Good thing she'd resisted even a snicker.

"Or maybe it was your kung fu pose with your hands out ready to chop bricks or boards or bankers' heads in half." Mrs. Whitmore patted Ellery's shoulder.

"Was it that obvious?" Whether the fight-or-flight stance had stemmed from the loan conversation or the threat of spending an evening with Allard Allman didn't matter. "What are you two doing out and about?"

"Testing my cousin's ankle to see if it's broken or whether he's going to decimate my speed records on the ski slopes like he threatened."

Cousin! What cousin?

"I'm a much faster skier than she is. Trust me. With or without an ankle."

Ellery gave a courtesy laugh, but only because she was still trying to process what Mrs. Whitmore had said. Maybe it was the confusion that caused her to blurt the question. Maybe it was foolish, impulsive hope. "You're not Mrs. Whitmore, his wife?"

"Me?" Mrs. Whitmore touched her chest. "Married to that guy? Ha! Fat chance!"

But they were both Whitmores, right? Their guest registration, the shared room, all clues pointed that direction, didn't they?

"Oh, I see how you could think that." Mr. Whitmore's upper lip curled. "But Freya's not just my cousin, she thinks she's also my nanny. And she gives terrible advice, while thinking of herself as my personal decision boss."

"Ha, ha," Mrs.—make that *Miss*—Whitmore deadpanned. Then she smiled at Ellery. "That's pretty funny, actually. We get mistaken for brother and sister all the time, and even for twins now and then, but never for a married couple. Call me Freya."

"You can call me Ellery, then." They seemed to be going the same direction, so Ellery walked up the street toward the center of town. They passed Mando's Electronics Repair, a ski equipment shop, and Newberg's Chocolates and Hot Cocoa Haven, which smelled like heaven would probably smell, if Ellery ever got there.

"And you can call him Bing."

"As in *I'm dreaming of a white Christmas* Bing? That Bing?" And *Holiday Inn,* and about a hundred other musicals like *The Belles of St. Mary's* with those accentuating-the-positive lyrics, and … Ellery slammed on her brain's movie-quoting brakes before she hurtled over the cliff.

"As in it's short for Bingham, but that second syllable's fighting words." Freya had a laugh like a ringing bell. "So I take it you're not married or that banker guy wouldn't be so forward. Although, that porter at the hotel mentioned you a little possessively when he brought up our bags."

"Lenny's heart would tempt unscrupulous gold miners to cut him open and pull out the nugget to sell at however-many dollars per ounce gold is selling for right now."

Bing stopped walking. "But you're not married to him." He hung back.

His position forced Ellery to turn around to answer his highly direct question. "Not to Lenny." Suddenly, visions of her bridal veil with the little satin rosebuds and pearls attached to the netting slammed her like a loaded freight train. "I mean, not to anyone."

Not to stupid Greg Maxwell. Curse him for making her chin tremble in front of these strangers after more than two years. Why had their failed wedding ceremony become the main topic of discussion in every beauty parlor and at every coffee shop in the county for months?

"I should probably let you guys go—" Ellery stared at the sidewalk, not interested in the pity that was probably in Freya and Bing's eyes. Fine, they probably hadn't heard her left-at-the-altar tragic tale, but the second they did, the pity would reside there. Just like it did in the looks she got from everyone who knew her. Even from Kit now and then.

Always from Mom.

A pair of women bustled out of the chocolate shop, laughing raucously. They bumped right into Ellery, shoving her against Bing's chest. She put up the palms of her hands to stop herself, and ended up grabbing onto his shoulders.

Whoa, those shoulders filled out the whole breadth of his coat.

"Excuse me," a chocolate shopper said to Ellery at the same moment Ellery said to Bing, "Excuse me."

Bing's leathery scent wafted in among the hot cocoa and the smoke from the local chimneys. No, Ellery took it back. *This* was what heaven would smell like.

She'd really like to get there.

"I'm sorry," she said, stepping back. "Like I was saying, I should let you two get on your way."

"And"—Freya's gaze flip-flopped between Bing's face and Ellery's—"I'm sure you have errands you're busy with."

"Thank you for walking with us a bit." Bing's jaw clenched and his temple pulsed. "You be careful around the bank, now, you hear?"

Ellery met his eyes. There was no hint of pity in his gaze. Smoke, yes. Deep, dark cocoa, yes. Something else afire, yes.

Something inside her ignited.

And he wasn't married. Looking into his eyes wasn't a sin. Heaven might be a fraction less unattainable, it would seem.

Other than the fact she shouldn't be looking at a guest with any kind of romantic interest. Speaking of ethics!

Ellery turned up the next side street toward the bookshops. She had to get her blizzard-like thoughts under control. Walk. Walk faster.

Nope, it was no good. A swirling storm of Bing Whitmore fell in frozen fractals all around her—credit to the Disney movie *Frozen*'s lyricists for the metaphor. Everywhere she looked, his face reflected up at her.

"And so I was telling JoAnn." One of the Newberg's Hot Cocoa

Haven bumping women loomed up half a pace in front of Ellery. "JoAnn, I said—"

Ellery barely slowed her pace in time to avoid ramming her in some accidental retribution.

Cocoa Woman took no notice, just blared on with her conversation. "We come all this way to Wilder River, and we can't even get a sleigh ride or carriage ride through the town? It's a blazing Christmas candelabra of disappointment if ever I encountered one. And do you know what JoAnn said?"

"What?" Cocoa Woman Two asked, possibly less horrified by the lack of sleigh ride than her friend was. "Did she freak out?"

"No, she yanked out her phone and started an *internet* search. How do I find the king or whatever of the Chamber of Commerce of this place? I'm voicing my complaint right now, she shouted!"

Cocoa Woman One's cackle at her own joke might not have been the catalyst for the break-off of the icicle directly overhead, but as it landed in a snow bank half a foot from Ellery's boot, it might as well have been a lightning bolt striking.

Sleigh rides. Yeah. Sleigh rides. With horses, and bells, and—

A hundred ideas bloomed in Ellery's brain at once, like a Christmas cactus in the sunlight of the windowsill of her mind. Possibly much faster than prudence permitted.

Much like her next words.

"Ladies?" Ellery caught back up to the women, who had moved on and were about to enter Barley Oats Bookshop. "Excuse me. I overheard your conversation."

"You're the girl with the hot boyfriend." Cocoa Woman Two grinned, lifting one wry brow. "If you get tired of him, let me know. He's hotter than that mug of steaming hot chocolate that left my tongue scarred for a week."

"He's not my—" No, that wasn't the topic right now. "About the sleigh ride. Or carriage ride, or whatever. I overheard your conversation. There *is* one. It's just taking bookings right now, but it runs on weekends. Can I take your names and put you in the schedule?"

She certainly could. Both of the Cocoa Women booked romantic rides two weekends out for themselves and their husbands, who, they said, weren't nearly as hot as Bing, but would do in a pinch.

"Great. Pickup is at the Bells Chalet. There's a deep discount for hotel guests."

"Bells Chalet? Shouldn't that be Sleigh Bells Chalet?" The cackling woman let loose, and two icicles fell.

Lightning bolts again.

Ellery thanked the women with an impromptu hug and a *Merry Christmas*. Then she literally ran all the way back to the hotel, barely avoiding slipping on ice.

"Guys!" she hollered. Great, now who needed the course in professionalism? Oh, who cared? "Mom! Kit! Lenny! Guys!"

They gathered. She spewed the entire plan to them. Well, at least the sketch of an idea she'd thought through so far. "What do you think?"

They liked it. Yes!

Sleigh Bells Chalet! It made perfect marketing sense. Much more marketing sense than the Southwest-theme décor and the dark purple walls in the lobby.

"I knew you'd come back with inspiration," Kit said. "I've got that fabric stash I told you about. We can Christmas-ify the lobby and all the bedspreads and throw pillows in the rooms."

"I gots paint out in the shed." Lenny aimed a thumb out toward his caretaker quarters. "You want I should paint the whole place white instead of this purple? Dark purple makes me think of bruises. And prunes."

"You have enough white paint?"

"Pops was always saying we was going to do the insides white, so I bought a lotta cans. I was just waiting on orders to start."

"You've got them."

Kit was already on the ground, prying up the edges of the faded carpet. "Yup. Hardwood underneath. That's what's to love about old buildings. When your Grandpa Bell bought it and renovated it in the seventies, the place was already fifty years old. He updated plumbing and electrical, but covered the floors."

And painted.

Deep purple.

"I know a guy with an electric sander. Big one. We can borrow it, I'll bet." Kit got out more than Ellery, which meant that unlike Ellery, she knew people outside the small sphere of this hotel. "This is going to be so amazing. And it won't feel like a crypt in here."

Crypt was an apt description. Ugh.

They'd need a *pardon our dust* sign to post. Not that there were many guests besides Bing and Freya to read it.

"What about a carriage? You don't happen to also know a guy with a carriage?" Ellery knew it was too much to hope.

That was the biggest kink in her plans. The most foolish element.

"If Kit doesn't, I do," Mom said.

"Mom? Really?" Mom for the win!

"Sure. My Uncle Wilbur always had one up in Pinetop. We probably only need to ask. Aunt Gilda won't be wanting it now that Uncle Wilbur has passed on. She doesn't like horses. More of a bingo night type of aunt, if you know what I mean."

Ellery knew Aunt Gilda—and her winnings pile from her time at the tables. "Could you call her? See what she thinks?"

Mom could. She went over to the desk to use the main phone to make the call.

Oh, man. Two weeks from now, she'd be the owner and proprietor of the newly, grandly opening Sleigh Bells Chalet, complete with weekend horse-drawn carriage rides and a renovated lobby, if not totally redone rooms.

"But—sweetheart." Mom put down the phone receiver in its cradle without dialing. "I can call Aunt Gilda, sure as you're born. But ..."

"But what? Do you think one of their kids took the carriage

25

already?"

"No, no. It's not that."

"Then what, Mom?" Please don't say Ellery needed a husband for this project. "It's vital to the survival of this hotel that we do something drastic—and immediate. This is my best idea, and the most economical. We've run through all the money I borrowed from Allard Allman at the bank. It would be like squeezing blood from a turnip to get it back from us now."

Not that she wanted Allard Allman squeezing anything near her, let alone her person.

"No, honey. It's—you don't know how to work with horses. It takes a long time to learn."

"Then I'll find someone who does and hire them to help us."

Mom, Lenny, and Kit all side-eyed each other.

"What? You don't think someone in this area with horse knowledge is in need of a job? Seriously? We're a horse community if ever there was one. Wilder River might as well be the featured music video for 'Home on the Range.'" There were seriously that many horsemen and horsewomen around. "We host three rodeos in the summer, don't forget."

"Maybe, but"—Mom winced—"you don't have any horses. Uncle Wilbur's were sold a long time ago. You don't have the first clue about how to even choose a team to pull a carriage."

Oh.

What kind of an un-chewable chunk of chocolate had she just bitten off?

"Then I'll find someone who does."

Chapter 5

Bing

"How's your ankle?" Freya might as well have had that question on one of those two-second video loops teenagers watched online while their brains rotted. "You ready to ski yet?"

"Let's just keep in mind whose bright idea it was to fill the entire bed of my pickup truck with luggage and who insisted I jump out over the side once it was all on the ground."

"Nobody made you jump. You were showing off."

"For you?" The two of them passed the fountain in the Wilder River town plaza. It wasn't running. It wouldn't be, not at these temperatures. But the lure of the hot cocoa scent from yesterday had Freya on a mission to return to downtown for breakfast. "No one else was around to see my daring feat."

"But, I'll bet all the presents under the tree, you *wish* a certain someone had been there to see it, had it ended in triumph instead of tragedy."

The chocolate shop was just across the street now. They paused in front of the town newspaper office to wait for a break in traffic.

"You are the least subtle matchmaker in the history of pushy cousins."

"You aren't denying that Ellery Hart is an attractive woman, though, are you?"

Why should he deny it? When she'd collided into his chest yesterday, that was the closest he'd been to an attractive woman in ages. His chemistry switch had flipped from the permanently-off position to full-speed-ahead the second her hands clamped down on his biceps. And she had the silkiest chestnut hair he'd seen since Rose Red's. Not that he was comparing that woman to a horse.

Okay, he was ridiculous. He could admit that.

"Look, she's pretty. But she's not interested in me. I'm a guest at her hotel." And Bing had a lot of emotional baggage to sort through before he'd be ready to worry about even making small talk with a woman, even a gorgeous one with deep brown eyes. More baggage than Freya had brought on this trip. "And I'm a deeply troubled person."

"There you go, living your life via the movies again."

"It's just as telling that you recognize the references."

"Ha! Not hardly as telling. I'm not the one spewing the lava of the lines from *Love is a Volcano.* You are." Freya smirked as the light turned red. "At least it wasn't a musical this time."

"Should have been. That movie would make a great musical. Or at least a stage production."

"What movie?" a woman's voice asked.

Bing turned to look. Speak of the angel, and she appeared. "Hey, if it isn't our host." The door to the newspaper office swung shut behind Ellery. "Getting a sneak peek of the local headlines?" He pointed up at the sign for the *Wilder River Rover* above them.

"Just placing an ad."

"Advertising is smart," Freya said as they scooted out of the way of the front door of the office. "And don't think I'm being critical, but does it make sense? I found your hotel in an online search. How effective is it to advertise the hotel to locals? The gymnastics shop, sure. They live here and want to enroll their kids in Constant Energy, but a hotel?"

"Here she goes again." Bing pulled Ellery's elbow slightly,

tugging her away from Freya. Into her ear he spoke *sotto voce*. "What did I tell you? She's forever giving the worst, meddling advice. She thinks because she has a doctorate in psychology that means she knows every twist and turn of the human mind—*and* all about hotel advertising."

"Bing! You can dial that snark down about three levels, thank you, very much."

Bing ignored Freya's protest. Ellery's shampoo infused his senses at this proximity. He nudged closer. "Don't let her uninformed opinions influence you. I'm sure you know what's best for your business."

Ellery laughed. It was the first time one of his jokes had hit a mark in a while. Her laugh was a rise and fall of birdsong. "Are you two in a constant war?"

They both shrugged. "Possibly," Bing said. "If so, I am the clear winner of every battle."

"To put your mind at ease, Freya, no. I didn't buy a newspaper ad. A full-on ad campaign isn't exactly in the budget." She looked at her fingernails, the clean ones. Sans paint. "I was putting a hiring listing in the classifieds."

She looked worried. Yeah, he should have guessed the hotel might have a financial struggle going on.

"Hiring more help for the hotel?" he pried, even though he probably shouldn't. If she couldn't buy ads, how could she hire someone? Well, she knew her business.

Okay, maybe she didn't. The hotel and its parking lot had not filled up by a single room or vehicle since yesterday that Bing could detect. Maybe the Bells Chalet's appeal for being quiet stemmed from its being totally empty. Probably not good for the bottom line. Shouldn't it be full this time of year? The streets were full of jalopies, skis, and poles strapped to the roll bars or out the back windows.

"Hey, I'm freezing. I'm going to catch this crosswalk light," Freya said, aiming a thumb across the street. "I'll just be meeting with a client online while I'm in the cocoa shop. Might take an hour. Come find me when you're done visiting, 'kay?"

"Fine." Bing shook his head. Sneaky, unsubtle matchmaker. "That's good, right? Hiring new people is a sign of business going well, right?"

"I hope so." Her lower lip tugged to one side. "If I can't find someone in the next few days, I'm going to be in a world of hurt."

"What kind of someone?" Bing stepped out of the way of a passing tangle of shoppers loaded with bags. He pulled Ellery aside, too. They were now in the little alcove of the entrance to the newspaper office, out of the wind. She stood close enough he could see a tiny chip in her right incisor. Otherwise, she had exceptionally nice teeth.

Oh, man. Was he assessing a woman based on the quality of her teeth?

"It's a long story."

"I have a long time. I'm on vacation, you know."

Ellery's eyes narrowed at him. She opened and then shut her mouth. Finally she said, "Would you like a guided tour of Wilder River?"

"Personally guided?" If Ellery Hart was his guide, then obviously, that was a yes. "Only if it's a walking tour. I'm trying to strengthen my ankle."

"That's the only kind our company offers, so you're in luck." Ellery didn't ask about how exactly he'd hurt his ankle, praise the stars above. "Would you like to see uptown or downtown?"

"Which one takes longer?"

"Downtown."

"Then I'll take downtown."

"Since it's the same fee for both, that's a good choice. You're a man who likes to get his money's worth."

"Yes, I do." And he had, when it came to horses in the Whitmore Stables. He'd bought and sold enough thoroughbreds in the past five years to make an exceptionally healthy profit for himself and all the Whitmore owners. "What's the fee?"

"There's a cost to everything, you know. The cost of this tour is you have to listen to my fictional histories for every place we walk past."

"Sold." Nothing he'd like more. "What's this coming up on our left?" They approached a standalone building with pillars and steep steps.

"That's the courthouse. The outlaw Jimmy Bilgewater was hanged right here on the steps for rustling bison out of Judge Carnahan's herd about thirty years ago."

"Thirty, eh?"

"Did I say thirty? I meant three."

"I can't believe that wasn't a social media sensation."

"Right? Well, small town events hardly ever make news outside the area." Ellery led him on through the narrow streets and alleyways of Wilder River. Every little place with any kind of unique architecture, she piped up with a crazy story. "And this here?"

Like a model on a game show waving to a contestant's new car prize, Ellery paused in front of a small green door.

"What about it?"

"It's the Green Door of Destiny. A direct portal to Disneyland. Saves tons on travel time down the coast."

"And on parking, I'll bet."

"Those parking fees are getting out of hand."

"Don't tell any of the other tourists. Some of them might quit skiing and head straight to the Magic Kingdom. The Wilder River economy needs their income."

"Your town's secret is safe with me." Bing pantomimed the zip-lip and the locking key. "I'm great with secrets."

"Oh, yeah? Me, too. Got any to share?" She lifted a brow over a twinkling eye.

No, he didn't. "Just the best-kept secret in the world: *buy low, sell high.*"

"Genius!" Ellery didn't seem disappointed he hadn't taken her bait to open up to her.

A tiny part of him kicked him in the shin for missing the moment. *She'd get my struggle,* the shin-kicker chided. *Mostly because I'm pretty sure she's got enough of her own problems that she won't sit around judging me for mine.*

Whatever. He wasn't going to tell her about Snow White. Or Rose Red. Or his cowardly flight of emotional burnout from Grandpa's legacy at Whitmore Stables.

"You never answered me about your classified ad." They'd come fully around the business area and were walking back up the main street. Newberg's Chocolate Shop might spew Freya forth at any moment. "What type of employee do you have to hire in the next few days—or else?"

That was basically how she'd worded it, right?

Ellery looked at him, as if to gauge his sincerity—and his trustworthiness. Not his teeth. After a moment, she heaved a sigh. "I might as well be frank. The hotel is not at its financial best, and I'm doing a major branding revamp. I'm changing its whole vibe."

"And you need a contractor? For the renovation?"

"Uh, no. Lenny is handling that. He paints, he repairs. We couldn't manage without the big old koala bear."

He did resemble a koala, now that she mentioned it. "So, like a branding specialist? SEO, advertising, and such?"

"Chuh! I wish." She looked so forlorn. Things must be pretty grim. "I've got to have something to advertise first. Meanwhile, I went a little nutso and booked a bunch of tourist experiences. About fifteen for the weekend after next. And it has brought in lots of guest bookings for then. Well, lots for us, I should say."

"That's good news, right?"

"It would be if I had the *faintest* idea how to accomplish it."

"What kind of guest-experience?"

"Horse-drawn carriage rides through town." She shudder-sighed. "I mean, I have access to a carriage. It might be in rough shape, though.

And I'm in the middle of the permitting process with the city. My grandpa was well-regarded, did a ton of service and community-building, so they're fast-tracking my application out of respect to his memory."

"The hotel was his?"

"Yeah." She looked at her feet. Most likely because she was going to lose the hotel, from the way it sounded. "But what I don't have is anyone to handle the horses."

Bing heard the final two syllables of that sentence, and then everything else she said got garbled and muted and indiscernible, like the dialogue of Charlie Brown's teacher. He shouldn't tune her out and make her inhuman when she'd been so nice, but Bing had shot down a long, metallic funnel, and was sliding fast.

"Well, don't look at me." He stepped away from her as quickly as he could. "I have to go now. Freya is probably done. See you later. And, uh, good luck with that."

His cowardly feet carried his yellow belly and his lily liver into the street. A single horn honked, and a jeep slammed on its brakes, but Bing didn't break stride or raise an apologetic hand—he just rushed into Newberg's Chocolate Shop, where he yanked Freya's phone out of her hand and her earpiece from her ear.

"Ouch! What are you doing?" she tugged it back, shoving her earpiece back in. "I'm sorry, Dr. Schaffhausen. My *cousin* is auditioning for a straight-jacket."

"This isn't funny, Freya. You're not with a client—or with a doctor, for that matter. I happen to recognize your movie reference to Dr. Emil Schaffhausen. *Dirty Rotten Scoundrels*? Do you have any idea how many times I've watched that show?" He pulled her to his feet and slapped a twenty-dollar bill on the table. "Come on."

"Where are you yanking me, may I ask? I'll go quietly, I swear." She held up her hands in peace. "Stop it, Bing. Did your witness protection ID cover get recognized? Are we on the lam again?"

"Not funny. We're going back to Massey Falls. I'm hiring a

temporary manager—for three months. And I'm selling my portion of Whitmore Stables. After that, you and whoever else can make decisions."

They were out in the winter sunshine now, and icicles dripped all around them. The temperature had risen in the time he'd been walking with Ellery Hart—harbinger of doom.

"Wait a red-hot minute, young man." Freya wrangled her arm free of his grasp and tugged her jacket down on her hips. "I booked this vacation on my own dime, thank you, very much. And I was just having a lovely conversation with the barista in there. Is that what you call a bartender in fancy coffee shops? Anyway, he was about to get my number—after his next customer—so I'm not leaving town until I get at least a day to see where it goes."

"Stop lying. You've got a doctorate. You don't seriously see yourself with a guy who makes hot drinks." He wasn't usually this classist.

"He's a school teacher. He's off work for Christmas vacation. It's his family's business. You, of all people, should know what it means to be *loyal* to a family business. Which is why you're being freakily ridiculous right now with this *get out of Dodge* rant. We're not leaving, and I'm not even going back to the hotel until after you do some 'splainin'. You were with Ellery Hart. How shocking could her good company be—unless it's the electric spark I saw zapping between you two every time you've chatted."

Freya was impossible. He didn't have to *'splain* anything. "I'm the one who brought you here, if you'll recall. I've got the truck and am heading out of this place post haste."

"If you'll recall, you gave *me* the keys, which are locked in the hotel room safe, and you don't know the combination."

Defeat.

"Now, spill it. All of it, including about Ellery."

No. He wasn't spilling it, and he wasn't staying in this place.

Most of all, he wasn't helping even the most beautiful, vibrant girl he'd ever met with any kind of horse problem. Ellery Hart could just forget it. And him.

And he'd forget her.

Chapter 6

Ellery

llery walked back to the Bells Chalet at top speed for a snowy day, avoiding ice patches, her hair still afloat from the wind coming off Bing Whitmore's violently fast about-face. What had she said to throw him into a tailspin?

It stung, whether she wanted to admit it or not. Hadn't they been clicking? Like faster than a telegraph's message?

Maybe she'd only imagined it. Just like she'd imagined Greg's commitment to her and to their relationship.

Why did she always do this to herself?

Whatever. She had too much to accomplish at the hotel with this renovation and with the impending guest onslaught to worry about Bing.

Even though Bing Whitmore was taking up the bulk of the available storage space in her brain.

Clear the cache. That was what she had to do. Now.

"Do you like it? The sign?" Lenny and Kit stood at the top of the steps. Lenny pointed over his head with his long arms to a freshly painted sage green sign with a blackletter style that read *Sleigh Bells Chalet.* "I hung it up there for you, Miss Ellery. Did I get it straight?"

"You got it perfect, Lenny! Who painted it? The calligraphy is incredible."

"Kit did it." Lenny squeezed Kit's shoulders. "She gots skills."

Yes, indeed. "I didn't realize how artistic you are." Ellery climbed the steps to inspect it a little more closely.

"Oh, I typed it with a cool font first, and then traced it the best I could."

But Kit had added shading, outlining, and a sheen to the brick-red lettering. "I love the gold leaf accent. It looks amazing."

Inside, lots more work was already underway. The lobby was a demolitionist's dream. Carpet gone, curtains eighty-sixed, the sofas nowhere in sight.

"I gots a roll-off out back and it's already more than halfway filled up to the top." Lenny beamed. "You want to watch me yank the carpet off the stairs?"

Whoa, whoa, whoa. "Uh, before that, can we double check if there's hardwood underneath?"

"There is," Kit reassured her, coming to her side. "The whole place is—top to bottom. But we should keep carpet in the rooms for now."

They didn't have time to refinish every floor in the place at once. "We should stick to the lobby for now." And maybe the stairway.

"What about the restaurant?" Mom asked, a tuft of carpet like a little oriole's nest in her hair. "Are we going to remodel it and open it, too?"

Oh. Ellery hadn't thrown that into the mix of this two-week whirlwind. "Too much to bite off right now. But maybe sometime?"

Mom smirked. "Okay."

Lenny and Kit worked the foyer. Ellery ran the electric sander for a while. It was coming along. Good thing their two guests were out for the day, or the noise and dust of the construction project would probably have driven them to check out for good.

If Ellery hadn't already driven them to check out by … whatever she'd said to make the guy bolt faster than Comet and Cupid.

Bing Whitmore was an enigma.

"I told you about the fabric hoard, right?" Kit came downstairs with an armload of folded linens. "What do you think of these for the sofas? I watched how-to videos all night on upholstery techniques, and I think I get it."

"Hey, that would mean we could save the couches and not have to buy new right now." Which they definitely couldn't afford. "I like this one." Ellery chose a deep red fabric that looked sturdy.

"Good. That's going to look great paired with this one for throw pillows." Kit held up a green plaid. "What do you think?"

"I think it's going to feel like a sleigh bells chalet in here in no time." She hugged Kit. "Thank you. So much! This is above and beyond, you know."

"Are you kidding? This is my dream come true." Kit clutched the fabric to her chest. "Every day I have been coming to work and looking around wishing I could have free rein to update."

Seriously? "I never knew."

"I didn't want to tell you. I know you love your Grandpa Bell, and this was his dream and his legacy to you."

Yeah. Very much so. "I like to think he'd love what you and Lenny are doing."

"If we can finish by the time the sleigh rides are booked, we'll be serious champs."

That was a big *if.* Two weeks for a major renovation of a space this size—they were crazy. They needed more manpower.

Ellery couldn't afford to hire anyone, not even the hostler she'd advertised for.

The bells on the front door jingled—they made so much more sense now that this was the Sleigh Bells Chalet—and in came their guests.

Freya and Bing dodged the cord on the sander and headed for the now-uncarpeted stairway toward the rooms. Freya waved in Ellery's direction, a sheepish look on her face, but Bing didn't even make eye contact.

Wow, Ellery must have really done something to irritate him. Which hurt a lot more than it probably should have.

Chapter 7

Bing

"**A**re you kidding me right now?" Freya stomped her foot. "Stop packing. You aren't leaving. Not after the way you treated that incredibly nice girl. She has been nothing but sugar and kindness to you, and you're acting like a crusty bear to her. All growly and snarly and ... well, jerkish."

"I'm going through stuff." He wasn't a jerk. And Freya shouldn't accuse him of being one. It was irritating and made him want to go crusty bear on her face. Couldn't Freya see he was *going through stuff*? "I'm not a jerk."

"You're doing a mighty good imitation of one. Ellery Hart would definitely agree."

Would she? Oh, geez. She probably would.

"You were out and out rude to her just now. You owe her an apology."

Well, he wasn't giving her one. "Not in this state of mind."

"It will make you feel better."

Would it? Possibly not. "Being rude isn't usually my default setting."

"Ever since Rose Red's accident, you've been on the razor's edge. But that's no excuse."

Fine. An apology to Ellery Hart might smooth over her feelings.

He'd hate to leave her feeling bad due to his prickliness. It really wasn't her fault he flipped out when he thought about dealing with horses. For pity's sake, Ellery Hart wouldn't be likely to even know that Bing even owned a horse, let alone the troubles they'd caused his emotional state over the past few months.

"If I dial down the porcupine and apologize, will you stop hounding me?"

"Yes."

"And will you let us go home?"

"That remains to be seen." Freya folded her arms over her chest. "It depends on your apology's effectiveness."

"You're not making it easy for me to resist resorting to violence."

"You don't have a violent bone in your body."

Probably true. But she shouldn't keep pushing to find out. Everyone had a breaking point. "I'll go apologize. But you promised to get off my case. Don't forget."

"Do you want me to come and observe, or will you be content to give me a play-by-play when you return?"

Bing shot her a look to let her know she was again pushing the limits, tugged his sweater over his head, and headed out the door of the suite and down the stairs to where the dulcet tones of a giant electric sander played on the winter air.

"Hi," he shouted, walking up to her. "Can I talk to you for a second?"

She wore clear plastic goggles, a dust mask, and a thick layer of sawdust coated all her visible surfaces.

His throat tightened. It was one of the most incredibly sexy sights he'd ever seen: Ellery Hart with full command of a power tool.

The sander's motor whirred down to a quiet roar. "Of course. Is the construction noise bothering you? We can resume it later when you're away from the hotel. We'd be glad to provide complimentary theater tickets, if that would compensate."

No, that wasn't necessary, and it had nothing to do with the noise.

"It's not a customer complaint. Or even a business matter. It's personal."

She blinked at him a few times from behind the plastic goggles. Was she going to listen to him or tell him to get lost like he deserved. Oh, she'd be polite about it, like telling him she preferred to keep all customer relationships professional, or something. But he had to hope she'd listen. He had to try.

At last, she peeled back the goggles, switched the OFF button on the power tool, and brushed off a tiny fraction of the voluminous dust coating her skin and clothes. "Maybe we could walk out back."

Sure. That worked.

She led him down a hallway beneath the stairs and out a back door to a fenced, open area he hadn't noticed before. "It's nice back here." There was a massive shed and some other kinds of out-buildings all painted neatly, a split-rail fence, and a huge field blanketed in snow.

"Yeah," she said, obviously not in the mood for raptures over the hotel's back yard. "What can I do for you, Bing?" She had that jackrabbit-like, skittish thing going on with her eyes, like the look she'd worn when he'd seen her trying to get away from that oily banker fellow.

Great. Was Bing now the creep she was dying to escape?

Freya had been right. He *was* a jerk, *and* Ellery Hart knew it, and she'd been hurt.

Great. He was blowing this whole thing known as human relations. And this after he'd botched horse relations, too.

"I owe you a huge apology."

"Okay." She looked at the ground. "Noted. I forgive you." She turned to leave.

"Wait." He reached for her but hesitated and didn't touch her. "Where are you going?" He wasn't through yet, at least it didn't feel like he'd achieved a full apology. Freya would not be impressed, anyway.

"I just have a big project going on in the lobby and there's a time crunch." She gave him another one of those scaredy-bunny looks. "Sorry."

"Ellery. I'm truly sorry." He quit mentally making excuses for his behavior—quit blaming his past experience on his present behavior—and just broke open. "I was a jerk to you. I want to do something to make it up to you."

"How about a nice review on TripAdvisor?"

"That's a matter of course." And not nearly enough to atone. "How about I help with your lobby?"

"You're a guest at the hotel. Guests don't jump in and offer to do manual labor. They're staying somewhere to be pampered. Or have you never been on a vacation before?"

"Actually ..." He searched her face, and in a few seconds it softened.

"You're being serious." Slowly she began to nod. "No vacation? Ever?"

He shook his head. "Not as an adult, anyway."

"Tell me." Her eyes tightened at the sides like she was processing clues in a mystery. "Are you here in Wilder River because your cousin is forcing you to take a vacation?"

Something like that. "I want to do more than *say* I'm sorry. You deserve better treatment than that. I'm good with power tools. I'm good with heights. I can roll a mean paint roller."

"Painting, eh?"

"Yep. And staining. I'm great with staining." He'd done most of the woodwork in Whitmore Stables when he'd first taken charge of the business. "It's in my blood."

"So, say I cut you open right here"—she touched his arm lightly—"Minwax English Chestnut two-three-three would ooze out, and not blood?"

Her touch sent repeating tremors up his veins. "Let me prove it." And his sincerity. "I'll help you prep the floors, and then I'll demonstrate my genius with transforming that wood grain from bad to blessed."

The rabbit skittered away from her face, and a side of her mouth tugged into a smile.

Cha-ching. He'd done it. Even Freya would approve.

But now, he couldn't leave.

***

Several days of sanding, sweeping, prepping, and staining sailed by. The work kept Bing's mind occupied. Well, so did being so near Ellery Hart all day long.

Anyway, the floors in the lobby and up the stairway looked better than new.

When the stain was fully dry, and the job was complete, Bing stood back and placed his hands on his hips. Not bad, if he did say so himself.

"I bow to your genius." Ellery came and stood beside him, her shoulder bumping his bicep. "You did not overstate your skills."

"Never."

"Once we get the oak finish stripped off the front of the reception desk, we can put a chestnut-colored stain there, and it will look worlds better."

Chestnut. Like her hair.

"Sounds really good."

That other girl, Kit, had already disguised the ugly pink and green tiles that were strung across the front of the reception desk. Each tile now was painted a Christmas color and had a little depiction of a silver bell with a red bow and some fir boughs.

The place was shaping up, but it still had a long way to go.

The only downside was with the changes, people would see this place in online pictures and they'd flock to its charm. It would no longer be the reclusive retreat he'd specifically asked Freya to book, and it could fill up overnight—and long before Bing's emotional regrouping effort had … regrouped.

"You're only a few steps away from being ready for a grand

opening."

"Don't fib. We both know it needs paint."

"Yeah, dark purple—with the dark floors—makes it a little …" He shouldn't say.

"Tomb-like?"

"I didn't want to use that term, but yeah. Maybe it skews more Halloween than Christmas."

"Boo!" She poked a finger in his ribs, and he jumped.

She didn't mind touching him. Huh. Working side by side with her all these days, that magical feeling he'd sensed on their walking tour through town hadn't reappeared—but that was obviously because he'd really botched that moment.

Maybe he could prove his trustworthiness if he kept on an even keel with her again today, and tomorrow, and … however long it took.

"Why aren't you using that restaurant?" he asked. It just sat there, looking forlorn through the french doors. "I mean, I've never run a hotel, but isn't a restaurant a chance for a side hustle, more or less?"

"That's what I was saying!" Ellery's mom, marched up. "I wasn't eavesdropping, I promise. Well, not much."

"Mom. We don't exactly have the capital right now."

"It wouldn't take much. What about something small?" the mom asked. She must really want to do this. "We could do hot cocoa, to stay in theme with the sleigh, at least."

"It just takes so much to get things in a kitchen up to code." She smirked. "And there's already a very popular hot cocoa shop in town, Newberg's." Especially popular with Freya, it would seem.

"But there's not really a code for hot cocoa, is there?" He couldn't imagine a code for cocoa. "Maybe he could check on that for Ellery. "Or for tea."

"Christmas tea!" Mrs. Hart went into a rapture. "People want tea all year round."

"Do you want to be the tea maker?"

If Mom's eyes had been the lights of a single Christmas tree before, now they were lit up like Times Square. "Me? I'd love that!"

"Christmas tea sounds great." Lenny walked up and placed a beefy hand on Ellery's shoulder. Maybe it shouldn't have bothered Bing to see another man touch Ellery. He wasn't dating her or anything.

But it did.

"I took home economics in college, you know." Mrs. Hart tugged on Bing's sleeve. "I have a knack for making tea."

Mrs. Hart's energy kicked into high gear. Suddenly, she couldn't wait to get this place done, and she was going to tell every single person there how to do it.

Bing walked out back toward the shed with Ellery. The yard near the shed smelled like motor oil, not horses. Thank goodness.

The air out here was bracing, but for some reason, it didn't bother Bing. *Maybe it's because I'm with Ellery Hart.*

"Looks like you've got yourself a Christmas beverage boss." He hoisted their totes full of staining supplies to put away. "An enthusiastic one."

"She will explode this from Christmas tea to wassail, and mulled wine, and spiced apple cider, and trust me. It won't end." Ellery swung wide the door to the dim shed.

"It looks like the idea made her happy, anyway." The sunlight fell in a shaft into the shed. The entire center was taken up by a gorgeous, vintage open carriage. White-painted with gold leaf, it had the scrolled ends of a Victorian sleigh. Large wooden wheels contained scores of spokes, shiny red paint on each of them. Red velvet tufted upholstery covered the seats.

And its axle was broken.

"Yeah, that was my fault." Ellery leaned against the ladder up to the shelves where they needed to store the wood staining stuff. "Lenny and I managed to load it safely onto the trailer and bring it down here from my Uncle Wilbur's farm, but when we were unloading, I steered wrong, and the one wheel slipped off the ramps, breaking the axle. Haste makes waste, they say. And they're right."

What a shame. "It's still pretty. You could park it in front of the hotel as a showpiece."

"Yeah, if I had another option for my carriage-ride bookings. I am so toasted on that."

Was her obvious stress level the reason she'd been less animated with him? If only he could chalk it up to that idea, and not blame his own history of being a jerk to her.

Ellery scaled the ladder, which leaned against the wooden shelving. "If I go up, can you hand me the box when I'm at the top? I'll put it on the shelf."

Sure. He could do that. And he could sneak a glance at her form as she climbed.

What? He was a guy—one who admired a stellar example of the female figure. Ellery definitely had one he could appreciate. Nice curve to her hips, nice sway of them as she climbed, nice—

"Oh, no!" she squeaked, as the ladder's feet shifted and it began to tip.

Bing lunged toward her, planting himself right in the trajectory of her fall. "I've got you!" He dropped the tote and put his arms out, cradle style, tensing them for impact.

Whump! The ladder toppled, and Ellery descended almost slow motion into his embrace.

Maybe it was an adrenaline effect, like he'd seen in his horses when they heard the starting gun and ran much faster than seemingly possible, but to Bing's muscles, Ellery was as light as a snowflake.

He pulled her close to his chest. "Are you all right?"

She exhaled loudly. "I should ask, are you?" She didn't climb out of his arms. Her heartbeat pulsed against his chest.

Bing was fine. The finest he'd been in a while, actually. Her gaze raked his face, and they shared the same steam of breath for a moment before she finally blinked.

"This floor is covered with stray rusty nails. If you hadn't caught me, I could have been in the ER for a tetanus shot."

Bing couldn't take his eyes off her to check whether the shed's floor was in truth cluttered with nails. All he could do was lock his gaze on Ellery Hart's face, smell her combination of shampoo, dust, and wood stain, and feel the throb of her pulse, which was quickly setting its time with his own.

"I'll help you fix the carriage." His promise outpaced rational thought. So did his next, very dangerous question. "What are you going to use to pull it?"

She blinked at him, her eyes tightening and then going wide. "Let's save that conversation for another time."

Huh. Maybe this woman really could *get* him.

"Deal."

Chapter 8

Ellery

Even with the door to the shed wide open and the Old Man Winter free to come and go as he pleased, the air somehow didn't seem as frigid when Bing was standing beside her.

The carriage was jacked up and stabilized, after only a few days' effort.

It looked good. Really good.

"The new axles are going to be safer for the passengers," he patted his handiwork like it was his teenage dream car and not a vintage carriage. "You were smart to change both of them at the same time. The old ones had rusted."

On his advice she'd done so. "You do realize that in a way, you're saying I was smart to follow your sage advice."

"If you want to put it that way." He shrugged. He was so cute when he wasn't being humble. Or at least he thought he was cute.

Which made him pretty cute.

Ever since he'd caught her when she fell from the ladder, something had flipped in her. She'd gone from being wary to trusting him. At least with physical things. He was strong, and he would protect her.

How long had it been since Ellery had felt even an inkling of that? Greg Maxwell might have made her feel that way, temporarily, but his leaving her at the altar had had a mind-wipe effect on any good qualities he may or may not have possessed.

So, maybe since before her dad died? Wow. That was a long time ago.

"Should we take it down off its jacks? See if your brilliant skills as a mechanic are as good as you claim—or if you've just been a young man fritterin' away your morning-time, lunchtime, dinnertime, too?"

"Are you accusing me like Harold Hill accused the kids in River City, Iowa?"

"Caught that, huh?" No way. Especially when it—embarrassingly—made no sense in context. "I don't know if we should give the quote five stars for being applicable to the conversation."

"No, but it had a rhythmic quality. And this carriage was probably built around the time Harold Hill graduated from the music conservatory at Gary, Indiana."

"Class of aught-five."

"Gold medal."

He knew this stuff. Revelation! Lightning bolts of it. Icicle-falling shards of it. "How do you even—"

"It's a gift. And a curse."

"Now, that's not a musical quote." Everyone knew the TV detective with OCD.

"Yes. Should we go on?" Bing crouched to loosen the bolt on the jack and crank it down. "For five points. It's a fine, fine day."

She knew this one—*Carolina*. Howard Keel's voice was liquid gold. "I'll say. Because they're harvesting the hay." She kind of sang it. Badly.

He courtesy-laughed.

Okay, so the man could name tunes from *Carolina* and quiz her on them. What man in his age group could do that? She had to reach out and steady herself on the shed's pillar post.

"Points to you," he said. "Your turn to test me."

She lobbed him an easy one, albeit from a cartoon. "The grass

49

blades are always greener."

"In somebody else's yard—*Good Neighbors*. But that's only a one-pointer. Come on, let's make it a challenge here, Ellery. You can do better than that." He cranked the jack down more, and the carriage slowly lowered onto its wheels, its springs creaking with a metallic whine. "Ready? Okay here goes for ten points. There's a noble stave o'er the family grave where my royal bones will stay."

No way. "You've got to be kidding. *The Crown and the Rose?*"

"You only get the points if you can name the next line."

She did. Easily. The part about the beautiful family crypt. "Morbid points for me. I'm ahead."

"That's only because you're sending me the easy ones."

"Fine. Twenty points if you can quote the Danny Kaye dialogue about the vessel with the pestle."

"I believe you mean the pellet with the poison."

"Where, exactly, is the brew that is true? I'd like to know."

With a gradually intensifying chemistry, they quoted the entire exchange from the classic movie about a court jester and his mistaken identity. Bing played Danny Kaye's part, and Ellery filled in all the other lines. Every time one stumbled, the other prompted. It took a while, but they got through the whole thing, even the bit about the flagon with the dragon.

"Pretty impressive," was all she dared say or she would have revealed just how little breath remained in her body.

Bing blinked at her, like he couldn't believe what had just happened any more than she could. So this was what the phrase *sharing a moment* meant. Bing's heart beat closer to hers in this moment than when he'd caught her in her fall from the ladder.

Holy roasted turkey with all the trimmings. I've met my old-movie-quoting male counterpart.

"So, who gets the point?" he finally said.

"It was my challenge to you. You get the points."

"Maybe we should share them."

Maybe we should share everything. She had to fight to keep her heart in check. "If you insist."

"Yeah. But we really should keep a running total for future challenges."

Bing's suggestion lit a sparkler inside her. There were going to be future challenges?

Speaking of quotes, C.S. Lewis once said or wrote something along the lines of it being a wondrous thing to learn there is someone else like us in the world, and that we are not alone. Ellery was much better at quoting movies than philosophers, but the purport of the professor's quote was palpable as the electricity that zinged in the air of the snow-covered shed.

Bing broke their gaze and ran a hand over the woodwork of the carriage. "Maybe we should test our work." Now that it was safely on the ground, they took away the jacks and put them back on their shelves in the shed.

"It looks absolutely ready to go." He patted the rim of the door. "Nice job cleaning up the upholstery."

"Not *quite* ready," she said.

He looked her way, his brows pushing together like he was going to disagree. "I've inspected this thing top to bottom. It's set."

"Yeah, well. Almost everything is set for next weekend. I've got ads running online, in the paper, and on fliers in businesses downtown. I've set up incentives with local restaurants and the playhouse to run a dinner-theater-hotel deal. To everyone's shock, I've even got a few skiers who booked nights in the upcoming weeks. It's a miracle. A Black-Friday-crowd-level of miracles."

"You don't *sound* like you're surrounded by miracles."

"Oh, I should, I know. I mean, look at the massive changes in the hotel that we were able to accomplish in a short time with even shorter funds."

"Total miracle. So what's got you down?" He sounded like he did care. Like George Burns said, once you can fake sincerity, the rest is easy. But was Bing faking?

Well, his hot-button topic was next. When she'd mentioned it before, he'd gone into full whirling dervish mode—points to her for the *Sound of Music* reference, even if it was only in her own mind.

Maybe Ellery shouldn't broach it, but he looked so earnest. Maybe this time he'd be okay. And time was crunching down on her, and she didn't have any viable options or anyone with whom to discuss her struggle.

"Frankly, I'm freaking out. I still have to make a huge investment. It's why we couldn't spend any money on the remodeling project."

"What kind of investment? I'm great with investments." He might have been off-quoting Tom Hanks in *You've Got Mail,* when he offers Meg Ryan advice like going to the mattresses.

"You probably don't know anything about this type of thing, so I won't burden you with it. You'd probably rather not hear."

"Try me. I have a surprising breadth of skills." He winked.

Flirting! He was flirting with her. Oh, goodness. Well, maybe she could venture into the topic. "I have over two dozen bookings for the carriage. And no horses."

A glower appeared instantly. "Oh," was all he said at first. "I ... actually ... I'm ... horses and I ... there's this history, and ..." The glower darkened, to a deep pewter. He fought it, and paced the length of the shed.

Ellery didn't interrupt. Clearly, a battle raged inside him, and she didn't want to get caught in its crossfire. *What kind of trauma has he endured?*

Bing came to a stop in front of her at last. He took a breath so deep his belly puffed out big as a Santa suit's belly. He let it out slowly. Finally, he said, "When it comes to knowing what horses to buy and not buy, I'm great with advice."

"*You've Got Mail.*"

"Ten points—and *you've* got my word. I'll help you, Ellery."

Chapter 9

Bing

What had Bing committed to?

Tomorrow. Horse shopping. Less than one day off. He couldn't even postpone the torture! Although postponing the inevitable would actually only prolong the agony.

The next morning came, and Bing still wasn't ready. In fact, he was less ready than he'd been yesterday—if that small of a measurement were even possible.

"I think I'm going to skip it." Bing paced the length of the executive suite he shared with Freya. Door to closet, closet to nightstand, nightstand to french doors dividing the two sleeping areas.

"Skip it?" Freya appeared at the glass doors, swung them open, and gave him the stink eye. "Bing. If you tread that circuit many more times, you're going to owe your gorgeous brunette friend Ellery new carpeting for this room. You're wearing a rut in it, dude."

Bing plunked his back against the wall, his hip hitting the console where the TV sat, jostling it. "What do you expect me to do? It's either pace or take a sedative."

"You're the one who promised to help Ellery Hart shop for horses."

"Don't remind me. I was out of my mind at the time. She had this whole lower-lip quivering thing going on, and all I could do was grasp at any way to stop it. She looked so forlorn, Freya. I was victimized."

Grabbing a blanket from the end of Bing's bed, Freya cozied up in the recliner. "If you want my professional opinion, this is the best thing that could have happened to you."

"Oh, so you're saying my having a total freakazoid meltdown in front of the most interesting, attractive woman I've met in a decade—or maybe ever—is the best thing that can happen to me? Because I'm dubious as to how that's a good thing, let alone the *best* thing."

Just like the psych professional cliché Freya could be, she lowered her glasses off her head and peered at him. "You have to face your fears. You can't run away from them."

"Nope. You used that Mother Superior voodoo on me last time. No instant replays."

"Then just think about it. You've got a massive hang-up going on, what with Snow White and Rose Red."

Duh. Except that maybe it wasn't all due to losing those racehorses. Maybe it was more due to the intense pressure of the business of thoroughbred racing.

"You're projecting it onto all horses."

Whatever. True. Fine.

"You're avoiding being around horses."

"Isn't that why we came to Wilder River? To get me away from work?" From horses, he should have said. And the chance of killing them every time he put them to work.

"You're building it up in your mind, possibly bigger than reality."

Two of the stable's best horses had been lost in a single year—one of them actually dying—and he was thinking about quitting the horse business. Was that blowing things out of proportion? No. "I think my reaction has been fairly proportional."

Freya went on like he hadn't retorted. "The worry of it is only going to grow bigger, the longer you avoid it. Yeah, the first time back around them after a hiatus is going to be bad. But I'm not telling you to go back to Whitmore Stables and immerse yourself in horse world again. All you'll be doing is dispensing some of your lifetime-of-experience-earned wisdom—*being there for*—the most attractive, exciting woman you've met in a decade. Or maybe ever."

Great. She was throwing his own words back at him. Using them against him. Why had he let her come along on this escape again? "And if I get some kind of panic attack?"

"You'll tell her it's food poisoning."

Lies. Yeah. That was the right way to handle things. "She does need some of my wisdom. That's for sure."

"And you're going to withhold it? Because you're …"

She didn't need to say the word *scared.* It pinged around the whole room like a pachinko ball.

"Bing?"

"What?"

"You're on vacation. You're not *working* with horses. It's going to be fine."

Yeah.

"Plus, you promised to help her."

Gah. She didn't need to remind him. But that lip-quiver popped into his imagination again on instant replay. Ellery really didn't have anyone else, or time to dig up anyone else she could trust. Horse sales were notoriously iffy. If Ellery Hart was working on a thin financial margin, like she said, and if he let her lose her investment just because he wasn't feeling like getting out there and keeping his word, then that really did make him the jerk he feared he might be becoming due to this so-called hang-up.

"You can get back to shrinking other people's heads now, Freya." He pushed away from his corner by the TV and walked out into the center of the room. "Mine's sufficiently decreased in size."

Freya muttered something that sounded like a dissent, but Bing was already out the door and heading down the stairs.

***

"Ready to head out?" he asked when he found Ellery in the kitchen area discussing tea-brewing tips with her mom. "Wow. You look really nice."

And she did. Her hair flowed over her shoulders in luscious deep-brown waves—shiny as a chestnut's shell. She wore a close-fitting royal blue sweater that brought out the color in her cheeks. A light danced in her eye when it landed on him.

At the sight of me? Wow.

"Thanks," she said, and her eyes dipped for a moment, making her thick eyelashes contrast with the cream of her skin. Cue the Hallelujah Chorus—she was gorgeous. "We're leaving now, Mom. Bing's helping me select the horse team. So we have to talk about your darjeeling and Earl Grey selection some *other* time."

Mrs. Hart got a sneaky look on her face. "He's a keeper, Ellery. Don't let this one get away. Not like the last one."

"Mom!" If looks could kill and if Truvie Hart were a cat, she'd be dead all nine times over. "Let's go, Bing. Before I do something the Romans would have rhymed with *mattress side*." She grabbed his arm, resting her hand in the crook, and they left through the back of the restaurant.

"Matricide, mattress side? Is that a quote from something?" He hadn't heard that one before. "No points for me."

"It's my own quote. And don't listen to her. Pretend she's mute."

Huh. So Ellery Hart had a fuse as well, eh? He wasn't the only one. He replayed the conversation and landed on her mom's final quip. *Don't let him get away, not like the last one.*

Clearly, Ellery had a secret in her dating past. Was now the time to ask? And if she were to tell him about it, would he be obligated to tell her about Rose Red and Snow White—his personal equivalent of an unfortunate relationship history?

She'd think he was ridiculous.

He didn't ask about any ex-boyfriends of Ellery Hart.

"I'll drive." He led her to the passenger side of his truck and helped her inside. It was kind of a leap for a girl her size. Freya barely needed the running board, but Ellery fairly had to jump once she stood on it. "Need a hand up?" He helped her aboard, at which she smiled down at him.

"Thank you. I could get a nosebleed at this altitude."

He needed a truck this big to pull the horse trailers. It wasn't just a symbol of his male ego. "It has to be tall to make room for the suspension—for taming all the bumpy back roads."

"I don't believe for a hot minute you'd take a truck this nice off-roading."

No, he wouldn't. "You got me." This was the Whitmore Stables truck. "For that, I've got a piece of junk I take in the hills. It's nothing like this truck, other than the color."

"I like black trucks," she said.

And I'm liking Ellery Hart more and more. Her sitting up beside him on the drive felt like they'd done it a hundred times before.

With the help of online maps, they found the farm where the first team of the day was advertised.

The farmer led them through the stables to see the team.

Bing stutter-stepped, but then crossed the threshold into the dim of the barn. He approached the team, and they nodded their greeting to him. Their eyes weren't bright, like the healthy horses back at Whitmore Stables. And they were much larger. Draft horses had a certain majesty in their height and breadth and strength that racehorses would never match.

Even less-than-impressive draft horses displayed that grandeur.

Bing admired the pair, despite their flaws.

"They're so pretty!" Ellery enthused at the pair of snowy horses with gray markings around their mouths. "I'm in love."

Ah, exactly. That was exactly how Bing felt every time he met a new horse, although probably not these horses, exactly.

Bing looked them over, asking a few questions. The farmer extolled their virtues, avoiding specifics.

"Bing? Can I buy them?" She looked up at him with anticipation dancing in not just her eyes but her whole body. "Can I?"

"Let the lady get the horses, brother," the farmer said. "I'll even knock off a couple hundred bucks, since I can see the lady will take care of them with love. Means a lot to a guy."

Bing didn't let his gaze graze the ceiling of the barn. "I don't think so, Ellery."

"Oh, but—"

He placed a hand lightly around her waist and whispered, "You did say you'd trust me, right?"

She nodded and turned to the farmer. "I'm sorry, sir. Thank you for letting us meet Blizzard and Frosty. They're beautiful."

"Oh, Bing." She looked so dejected. But she kissed the horses goodbye, and then Bing helped her back into the truck and drove down the gravel drive before she huffed out her complaint. "Seriously? They were perfect, and he was going to give me a discount. Can't you imagine how pretty my carriage would look when pulled by a team of snow white horses, one of which is more like milk?"

Ah, an *Oklahoma* reference. Knowing the surrey with the fringe reference probably earned him some points, but he didn't feel like he'd won anything. Not until she understood his reasons for yanking her out of there. "They were indeed beautiful. While Rogers and Hammerstein would've *wisht* that ride to go on forever, with those two, there was no way."

"Why not? They definitely looked big enough to pull my carriage."

"Draft horses might not be my first area of expertise, but I know a sway back when I see one." The spine could have hosted a thrilling roller coaster. "Plus, the owner refused to provide any veterinary records."

"But we could get those from the vet, surely."

"When I asked, the owner said he didn't have a consistent caregiver for the horses, which was a big red flag."

"But he was so happy I was taking them to a good home. Surely, he loved them. They were lovable horses."

Faked. Pretend love. Bing had loved horses, and he knew what that emotion looked like. "But the kicker? The guy wasn't going to let you take a test run with the team in harness. That was the third strike."

He almost said nail in the coffin, but then an image of Snow White, down on her side, flashed behind his eyes. The truck swerved, but he got control of it again. "Sorry."

"You protected me, then"—she said as if slowly realizing he'd been motivated by good, not evil—"from my enthusiasm and lack of information. Thank you."

A deadly combo. "It was no big deal."

"To you, maybe, but it's a big deal to me."

"Don't mention it."

"No, Bing. I didn't want to ask for help from anyone. I don't want to borrow, or to owe, and I am really determined to keep Grandpa Bell's dream off life-support—without dragging anyone else down in the process. But I could have sunk everything in a hot minute without your advice. So, thank you."

"That's the reason I'm here." Was it limited to that reason, though? Not entirely. He was here for a lot of reasons. More growing every hour he spent with this fiery, energetic, driven but sweet woman. "Should we check out the next team?"

They did, and a third and a fourth. Problems with all of them.

Problems, yes. But something about them ... Bing's soul chased a will o' the wisp of a hope flitting off into some darkened part of his soul and lighting it up. Something about the draft horses he was viewing felt different.

Ellery bent over and put her head in her hands. "I'm starting to think we're never going to find something. Maybe I'll need to cancel the bookings for next weekend." She tipped her face toward him, and that chin looked like it could start to tremble again any second.

"Don't do that just yet." He couldn't let that happen—the cancellation or the chin trembling. "Let's at least check out this last team. The dealer said he's offering Clydesdales."

59

"Let's hope these are my pair."

Bing parked the truck and helped Ellery down. They met the owner who took them to the team in question.

"What are they called?" Ellery asked. "They're gorgeous."

There she went again, enthusing. But this time she might be right. Depending.

Tall, with sleek black coats and a long fringe of white around their hooves, Donner and Blitzen were a fine match.

"How old?" Bing asked the dealer. Both horses' ears lifted and pointed in Bing's direction, as though they'd heard his voice before and recognized it.

"Nine, the both of them."

A good age.

Bing inspected further. Sleek coats. Good teeth.

"They're enormous," Ellery gushed. "They look like they could pull an army tank, not just a romantic carriage."

Bing wasn't so immediate with his praise, at least not vocally. He walked around both horses, inspecting their teeth, their legs, their hindquarters. He looked in each of their eyes.

These were the horses Ellery needed.

Bing patted Donner's neck. Blitzen wuffled and gave a deep nod, as if he'd read Bing's mind. Donner wuffled next, and then placed his huge head beside Bing's, as if to whisper in his ear—as if to say, *"We're the horses you need, Bing Whitmore."*

Bing took a quick step backward. *I'm done with horses.*

But was he? Draft horses and thoroughbred racing horses existed in wholly separate spheres. Grandpa had loved racing life. It energized him. All it did for Bing was translate to soul-crushing stress, especially when something as dramatic as broken legs were such a frequent occurrence. Especially when Bing was so personally invested and connected to the individual horses.

Could he love a horseman's life in some other way?

I'm not ready to decide.

That didn't change the fact that Ellery needed advice on her team.

The dealer stood back, arms folded across his chest, poker face.

"How much?" Bing asked at last. The dealer named a price. "We'll discuss."

Bing took Ellery on a walk around the dealer's parking lot.

"It's a good buy," he said when they were out of the dealer's earshot. "I checked these sellers out, and they have a good reputation."

"But ..." she said, a hitch in her breathing.

"But what?"

She bit her lower lip. That stopped the sudden tremor. "Bing, it's more than I had been planning to spend."

Oh. That was a consideration. He had no interest in breaking her bank account. "Maybe, but when someone buys a horse or a team, it can be an investment. This team will be gentle, easy to train with your carriage—since they've been yoked to one another many times in the past. They're a good age, and I can tell from several inspection points that they've been treated right." Not to mention, their veterinary records were impeccable, and the dealer demonstrated them in harness together. It was a no-brainer.

Except the money. He shouldn't pressure her. "The other option is to find a team and rent for a while. What are your bookings like? How often are they going to be used?"

"Daily. Multiple times a day. At least from what I can tell so far. At least through March when the snow starts to melt. Then, there should be springtime trips around the lake for viewing the wildflowers."

Then renting didn't make as much sense. He looked up at the snow-laden clouds. "You'll have to make the decision."

"If you say they're right for me"—she took both his hands—"and for the Sleigh Bells Chalet, I'm going to trust you." She raised up on tiptoe and kissed his cheek.

The kiss soaked into him, past the layer of pain he'd assumed was impenetrable, and infused his inner workings. It burned, but only for a second before transforming to a warm blanket on a subzero night.

The dealer walked up. Ellery let go of Bing's hands and turned to the guy.

"My friend says I should take them."

She called him her friend! Not her hotel guest. Plus, she was taking his advice? He wouldn't let her regret it.

"Your boyfriend knows his business." The dealer gave a head-nod.

"Oh—he's not my—"

The dealer interrupted her protest. "I recognize you from somewhere, don't I?"

No. Not here. He wasn't ready to talk shop about racing or thoroughbreds or anything of that nature. Not now, while inspecting horses on Ellery's behalf.

"Har. I get that all the time. I've got one of those faces."

The dealer laid off the topic and went to work finalizing the sale—and even offered to deliver the horses to Wilder River in the morning, once Ellery had made arrangements for how and where to stable them. They shook on the deal, and then signed on the line for Donner and Blitzen, the sleekest ebony team Bing had seen in a month of Sundays.

And the key to your healing, something whispered. He batted it away.

"This makes me a horse owner, I guess."

That made two of them. Not that he'd told her so. Maybe he should. Shouldn't he? It might get weird if he didn't tell her anything real about himself soon.

Chapter 10

Ellery

Whew, I'm glad that's over. Ellery climbed up into the truck with Bing's help, his fingers' warmth leaving a residue on her skin. "Donner and Blitzen, huh? Thunder and Lightning, translated. Let's hope that's not the case. I doubt hotel guests are looking for a stormy ride in a romantic carriage."

"Either way, much preferred to Prancer and Vixen, if you ask me." He turned the key. It clicked a few times before he fired up the diesel engine.

"It's a lot of money, but since you're so confident, I actually feel good about it." She settled back against the seat of the truck and hugged her legs to her chest. Too bad this truck didn't have a bench seat. Shopping for the team had chilled her to her bones, and she could have used a body heat transfusion from a big, warm-hearted guy right about now.

"No buyer's remorse?"

"Surprisingly, no." She let out a long sigh.

"What's wrong?" He was asking, but did he really want to know?

"Oh, nothing. Except that I don't know how to work horses, and barely how to feed them, let alone care for them. Now that I own Donner and Blitzen, I will have to hire someone for real to drive the team with the carriage. I don't exactly trust myself with that task. Plus, I kind of need to run the hotel."

"Can't be out gallivanting in the snow all day with the horse team and carriage." His voice grew tight, as if he didn't want to be doing it either. Which—it didn't make sense. A guy with as much know-how about horses as Bing shouldn't have been avoiding them. It didn't add up.

"Have you had any responses to your oh-so-modern ad in the classifieds?"

"Believe it or not, I have."

"No way. Unbelievable. Completely."

She chuckled and slapped his upper arm with the back of her hand. "Geez. What do you think? Of course the *Wilder River Rover* also has an online platform—where they list their classifieds."

"Oh, that makes a lot more sense. Otherwise, the main readership responding to the ads would be out of the age range for the job you need to fill."

"Are you saying only old people read the newspaper?"

"I'm saying only old people look for jobs in the newsprint. Everyone else looks online."

True enough.

"So, there was more than one response?"

"About fifteen, believe it or not. I chose seven to interview. They'll be coming in tomorrow afternoon." Where she would have to go on a gut feeling about whom to hire to take care of her insanely pricey investment. How on earth would she know whom to trust?

"What kinds of questions are you going to ask the candidates?"

This was crucial, obviously, but she had no clue where to even start. "What would you suggest?"

"Oh, I don't know. Experience riding, temperament, experience with teams? Knowledge of how to put them in harness?" He went on a question-listing tear.

"Whoa, my friend. Is this your way of saying you want to sit in on the interviews?" If he would, that would take so much pressure off her—and cut down the fear of the unknown by a huge amount.

He didn't answer at first, but finally he said, "Donner and Blitzen are pretty special. You can't have just anyone taking charge of them. You're going to want to see your top picks interact with the horses, as well—and keep a close eye on that."

All good points. All points she'd never have known without his advice.

"Okay, Mr. Horse-Knowledge. If you've got time tomorrow afternoon, I'll put your name in ink as the second interviewer."

"Time?" he grinned. "Mr. Horse-Knowledge is on vacation, remember? He's got nothing but time."

Maybe, but Ellery was starting to see that Bing Whitmore possessed a lot more than mere time.

And all those qualities were starting to become irresistible—even though he was a guest in her grandpa's hotel.

Chapter 11

Bing

"She bought the horses I recommended." Bing paced between the tables of the mostly empty bistro. Soon the dinner crowd would come in, and he'd have to stop, but for now, he weaved his way between three nearby tables. "I might have spent her into the grave."

"Why didn't you just spring for the team?" Freya turned on her bar stool. "You could probably buy your sweetheart hotel owner five crack carriage-pulling teams and not even see a blip in your monthly budget."

True. Bing could have sprung for a dozen teams for Ellery Hart and her carriage venture without batting an eye. Grandpa's thoroughbred legacy wasn't anyone's idea of chump change. "Ellery Hart wants to be self-sufficient." She'd even said so.

"Maybe she claims that, but most girls want to be taken care of."

Not this one. At least that wasn't how he read her. "I can give her advice, but not the team."

"Why not?"

"Because she's going to come out of this brush with financial death victorious—on her own. If I give her stuff, then it cheapens her triumph. Ellery Hart deserves all the thrills of that victory."

Freya nodded, like she knew his deepest secret. "I see. You're saying Ellery Hart deserves everything good."

"Precisely." Bing started pacing through the chairs and tables again. *I want Ellery to have all the good things she deserves. Am I the man to give them to her?*

"What about the best carriage driver in a hundred-mile radius? Does she deserve that?"

"Of course."

"By that you know I mean you, right?"

Bing bumped a table with his thigh, tipping a sugar shaker. "Shopping for a horse team is one thing." He righted the sugar shaker, but it kept toppling. "Actually driving the carriage is a lot more interaction."

"Right." Freya's elongated *i* in *right* always rubbed him wrong.

"Look, Freya, I'm making progress. But I'm not there yet."

Freya gave a little excited golf clap. "Oh, listen to you using that hope-filled adverb: *yet*." Freya stood and tugged him over to her table, where she pushed a bowl of soup at him.

He stared into the bowl, like it was tea leaves and held all the answers. Finally he lifted a spoon to take a bite.

"Does this *yet* word mean that you think *sometime* you're going to be okay to come back to your life again? I have some clients who are tired of meeting over the internet."

The soup was good. Minestrone with extra oregano. "What it means is I'm done shopping for a team, and I'm not driving her carriage."

But was that all it meant? Something about Ellery's brief kiss on his cheek had cracked through his hard candy shell. Okay, it probably wasn't a candy shell. And he was more cayenne than milk chocolate on the inside. Except around horses, when he became marshmallow fluff.

Oh, what was with the snack analogies? He shook them off and unwrapped a cellophane packet of saltines to counteract the sugary dumbness.

"Fact is," Freya said between gulps of her beverage, "that in the psychology world we'd say you accomplished something major today.

You're the one who should be taking the victory lap."

"Me?"

"You faced down a situation fraught with triggers. And you didn't buckle."

Yeah. Okay. Maybe she was right. He'd manned up, for sure. "Fine. Good. This calls for a celebration dinner."

"Yes!" She reached over and pushed his arm. "Now you're getting the idea, cousin."

"Where do you want to go? There's a steak place up by the ski slopes I hear has a mean prime rib and the world's best homemade bread."

"You know I love a good cut of meat, but sorry. Not tonight, pal."

Uh, was she blowing him off the second she'd set him up for inviting her to dinner? "Uh, aren't you the one who suggested a celebration?"

"Sure, but I've got a date. And so should you."

"A date! With whom?"

"With Ellery Hart, duh." Freya drained her glass and set it down with finality. "Why are you even asking that? You want her so much you can hardly breathe. It's getting ridiculous to watch you dance around your palpable ache for her. Just take her on a date and kiss the living daylights out of her already."

"I *meant* who is your date? Geez. And let's keep the living daylights safely inside Ellery Hart. She has a lot to accomplish in the next few weeks, and she wouldn't want to miss it."

"See? You're already putting her needs and wishes higher than your own on your priority list. It's so *sweet*." She hung on the *e* in sweet, just to mock him. He crumbled three saltines and threatened to toss them in her hair. "Hey, knock it off." Freya shooed his hand away. "And my date is with the hot bartender in the hot chocolate shop. We're going off to do hot yoga."

"Hot bartender, hot chocolate, hot yoga. Aren't you going to overheat?"

"Oh, I sincerely hope so." Freya shook the ice in her glass. "In a chaste and moral way, of course. I'm possibly his shipoopi."

"Third date kisser. Got it." He subtracted points from Freya's score for reusing too many *Music Man* quotes and not branching out to other musicals. "At least you're not a girl who *cain't* say no." There, he mixed it up with *Oklahoma.*

Although, he'd used that musical with Ellery yesterday in the surrey with the fringe on top reference.

Ellery was creaming him in the movie-quoting scoreboards. He needed to catch up with her.

Maybe over dinner.

No sense celebrating his victory by eating alone. Even if he couldn't exactly explain to Ellery why it was a victory dinner.

"Fine. I'll call her."

"It's about dang time." Freya air-kissed his cheek and headed out of the bistro to prep for her hot, hot, hot date.

Bing dialed Ellery, but he got no answer. He ate a few bites of his soup, but it was cold now. Before he could take it to the counter and ask for them to heat it up in a microwave somewhere, up walked Ellery.

"Hey, what are you doing downtown? Did you know how to find me? I was just trying to call you."

"What for?" She handed a credit card to the cashier, who gave her a stack of Styrofoam take-out boxes in a sack. "I had my phone off while I was in a staff meeting powwowing on grand-opening strategies. I promised them lunch, so I've got to get this stuff back, or Lenny's stomach will stop merely threatening with its growls and actually break out and attack us all. Sorry. What's going on?"

"Would you like to go to dinner with me to celebrate—er, buying Donner and Blitzen?"

"Like, as in … a date?"

Sure, of course a date. "Is that not kosher?"

"Um, you're a guest at my hotel."

"Is there some kind of ethical rule against dating a guest? I mean,

69

I've heard of boss-secretary concerns, but never anything to worry about in this situation." Was he putting too much pressure on her? "If you like, we can call it a business dinner. Or even an appointment, if that's better."

"Well"—she looked at her shoes and then back at him—"I guess that would be okay. As long as we keep it professional."

"Why wouldn't we?" Other than the fact that Freya was a hundred percent accurate in her assessment of his aching desire for this woman. Every little thing she did was magic, and a British pop song from the early eighties could quote him on that. "I'm completely professional."

"A professional what? I don't even know what your job is."

Maybe they should discuss that over dinner. "I'm buying. Do you like prime rib?"

"More than practically anything else in the whole world!" She laughed. "But that's an obscure quote. If you can get it, that's an automatic win for you and game-ender."

He wasn't ready to end the game, so he didn't say he recognized the quote from the 1995 wry British comedy *Cold Comfort Farm*. "No idea."

"Never mind. I do love prime rib, and I'm starving. Buying horses is hungry business." She took her card back, and the cashier handed her the bagged meals.

"Want a ride?"

She did want a ride. Bing drove them up to the ski resort area, and pulled into the parking lot of the hotel again.

"I'll see you tonight," he said as he went upstairs to make a reservation at Optimus Prime Rib. Even if it was only a so-called *appointment* in her mind.

Come on, it was a date.

***

He couldn't have chosen a better restaurant if he'd lived in the area all his life and done extensive testing. Outside the place, the mesquite smoke from the grill permeated the air. This was going to be good.

Inside, the romantic ambience was perfect: ski lodge with windows practically to the sky, table for two with a view of twilight on the slopes, the snow faintly pink—just like the blush on Ellery's cheek and the color of her v-neck sweater.

A candle flickered between them, surrounded by some holiday greenery, and the cathedral-ceilinged room smelled faintly like the bonfire burning in the giant, stacked-stone hearth a short distance away.

"You come here often?" It was the cheesiest line known to man. Why was he suddenly awkward?

"On all my non-dates, naturally." She perused the menu.

Date equals awkward. That had to be his problem. Maybe he should think of it as an appointment, too, just to reclaim his chill, manly vibe.

"Congratulations on becoming an official owner of a horse." He lifted his water glass, and she toasted. "It's a great way to live."

"I'll soon find out."

Great. She hadn't taken his hint. He'd have to lay it on heavier if he were going to be candid with her about his job. "Did you ever have a different job, like, before taking the reins at the Sleigh Bells Chalet?"

"I see what you did there. Reins? Good one." She toasted to that one, too. Good thing they only had water. At this rate they could be tipsy before they even received the basket of bread. "Yes, I spent a couple of years in an accounting firm in a city called Reedsville."

"That's not far from where I live. Together with Torrey Junction, Reedsville, and my town—Massey Falls—the three cities make a triangle."

"Massey Falls, huh?"

"Heard of it?"

"It sounds familiar. I spent a lot of time with my face in a ledger."

"What brought you back to Wilder River from there?" He was getting nowhere. She hadn't picked up on his vague allusion to the Torrey Stakes racetrack, so he couldn't segue into his profession. Did she really not want to know? Maybe this was actually a business dinner in her mind. Nothing personal. "Did you come back to work at the hotel?"

"Uh, no." She looked out the window at the ski slopes. Lights came on along the cables of the lift. They sparkled against the snow. "I came back for a guy. I know, I know. It's a total cliché. Quit your job and move across borders to chase your high school sweetheart."

"I take it things didn't go as planned."

"Oh, they went exactly as I always dreamed—at first. Right up until the wedding day. Me in my gorgeous dress, in the veil with the little satin rosettes studded with pearls. Unfortunately, Greg Maxwell never made it to the church."

Whoa. Stood up—like, on the day of days. "That completely reeks. I'm talking, potatoes-gone-bad-under-the-sink-for-a-month reeks."

She stared at him for a while, a bunch of emotions fleeting across her face, none of which he could precisely pinpoint. At least one was pain. Another was relief. "Yeah. Reeks pretty much covers it."

"Where did he go instead?"

"Besides to the fiery blazes according to all my ranting days after the wedding? Besides *not* to the bank to pay me back for all the money I blew on said-wedding? I don't really know. I wish it had been to personality and life-choice rehab—but before I'd taken his ring."

"In a way, sounds like that was a narrow escape."

"I like that phrase better than close call." She drank another swig from her water glass, crunching the ice. "What about you? Any close calls or narrow escapes?"

Now. He might as well tell her now. "Just with a couple of females I may never get over."

"Oh." She set her glass down, and then smoothed her napkin on her lap a few times. "That's sad to hear."

"It's even sadder if you know they're both fillies."

"Fillies." She blinked.

"I mean actual fillies, not some weird teenage-cowboy moniker for a young woman." He was rambling. He'd better nail his point now or he was never going to. "One was a thoroughbred racehorse named Snow White. She won the Torrey Stakes last May, right after winning two other big races. She was Whitmore Stables' best hope for getting into the larger circuit, along the lines of Belmont or the Preakness."

"Was? You're using the past tense."

"Six weeks after her amazing win, and right before we were set to transport her to another big win, she fell. Tumbled, really. Broke her leg during a regular canter around the track. It was so unexpected, not even in racing mode." His voice was tight, and he knew it, and he didn't know how to loosen it up. "They couldn't save her."

"Were ... were *you* the one riding her at the time?"

It was a detail he never, ever mentioned. Not even to family. They all just assumed one of the stable's horse trainers had been on Snow White during the fall, but Ellery Hart had divined his true source of pain in an instant. He closed his eyes and gave his shallowest nod.

In a split second, her hand had shot across the table and encompassed his, pressing hard, imbuing him with a tenderness and a compassion he hadn't felt from anyone—not even himself—in months. That grasp suffused his whole being. A dark ghost detached itself from somewhere inside his ribcage and floated up into the rafters, and then out into the dimming night.

"You must have been tortured by that."

"It would have been easier to get over if—" He knew it would sound melodramatic to tell her the second part of the story. It would sound like he was making it up.

"No, something like that stays with you for, well, forever. You loved that horse. I get it now that you could see that love—or the lack of it—in the eyes of that farmer selling us those white horses. It's clear as a church bell on Christmas morning that Snow White meant everything to you."

"I did love her. Not just for her potential as a racehorse. For her soul." His ankle still smarted from the accident. The tossing of luggage and jumping out of the back of his truck onto the ground on the day he and Freya had arrived in Wilder River hadn't been the source of his sprain, but it had definitely renewed it.

So, yeah. He'd been a little snippy about the situation. Not that he should be making excuses for bad behavior, but he had one, if anyone ever asked.

"I'm sorry. How have you handled the loss?"

"Well, at first, she had a potential successor by the name of Rose Red."

"*Had?* Again with the past tense? Tell me she didn't die, too!" Ellery clutched her heart with both hands, her dark brown eyes flying wide. "Oh, no. Please."

"Rose Red is alive."

Ellery's smile grew, and then faded. Her shoulders fell. "But from the way you stated it, I take it something happened to her."

"In a freak, repeat accident, Rose Red also had a fall. Not the same way. She was in a timed trial race at the track, being ridden by one of the stable's trainers."

"Not you this time."

No, he hadn't been on a horse. Not since Snow White. He shook his head. "But her leg broke as well. Fortunately, a young country vet was able to set it soon enough that her life was spared. Of course she won't ever race."

"But at least she's alive."

Yeah. That mattered. A lot. He was so grateful to Dr. Wilson for taking a risk and saving Rose Red, at least for a while. The horse's life would always be tenuous.

"Do you miss her?" Ellery whispered.

"Every single day." He looked at his plate. "The world is emptier without Snow White in it." He turned his hand over and interlaced his fingers with Ellery's. They fit nicely.

Perfectly.

Being able to tell someone about this, someone who really seemed to *get* his emotional investment—and didn't just try to psychoanalyze him, thank you very little, Freya—loosened tight knots all over inside his being. Ellery Hart was slowly and surely taking possession of his heart.

One of the fire's logs crackled, cracked, and fell, sending sparks up the chimney flue, in nature's echo of the sparks flying up through Bing's body. Every second that he shared sensory contact with Ellery, those sparks ignited more and more little corners of his soul.

I could burst into full-on conflagration at this rate.

"I don't know if they're ever going to bring our menus. Would you like to walk on the deck?" Out on the deck, he could touch her more. "I know it's cold."

Ellery blinked at him. "I highly doubt I'll notice."

Bing jumped to his feet and helped her out of her chair. *Neither will I.*

Sliding glass doors led onto the deck—just as the waitress walked up with menus.

"We'll be back. Can you save our table?" he asked as he led her outside, where he took her in his arms. "Ellery Hart?"

"Yes?" Her chin tilted upward. Despite her assertion, she did shiver. They hadn't put on their coats and only wore their layers of shirts and sweaters against the chill.

"You're cold." Bing, too, shivered—not necessarily from the shock of icy air with each breath. This woman had him electrified.

He pulled her close. "Is that better?" They were alone on the deck, just the two of them under the starry skies.

"Almost." Her voice grew sultry. In the evening light, her eyes dilated, and he could have fallen into their inky depths. "Closer," she whispered.

Oh, he could do closer. He tightened his arms around her shoulders, pressing her softness against his torso. She smelled like flowers, even in the smoke-tinged night air of this mountain town. He pressed his nose into her silken locks, closing his eyes just to inhale her irresistible femininity.

"Even closer," she whispered, letting out a little sigh when he embraced her flush against his chest. Their gazes locked, and their breath synchronized. "Bing," she whispered, her whole body becoming supple in his embrace and turning all the icy air around them to fire.

He met her softly parted mouth with his own.

Kissing Ellery Hart was like a ride on the fastest thoroughbred down the steepest hill with no bottom in view. The whoosh of the race deafened him, and he heard nothing, felt nothing else. Nothing existed but this kiss, this dive into the depths of their connection.

Every pass of her velvet lips across his shot him farther and farther into the land of no return. A brush of her cheek, a wisp of her breath, transported him from wonder to wonder and from wish to wish, desire to desire—as her hands ran up his spine, across his neck and through his hair.

"I think I wanted this before I even met you." She was what he'd been missing, know it or not. "That man who left you at the altar was a fool. How could he miss out on this?"

She gasped and pulled away, allowing a frigid wall of air between their bodies. "He had a good reason," she said.

Chapter 12

Ellery

I'm kissing Bing Whitmore. We're kissing like nothing else exists. Oh, merciful brown-paper packages tied up with string.

Bing Whitmore was all of her favorite things.

More than that, kissing Bing Whitmore was like free-falling. His lips erased Newton's laws for her internal organs, throwing them into zero gravity, and spinning Ellery off into a tumbling flight through a crystal-studded tunnel across the galaxy.

Until, that rocket-ship ride clunked to a halt. Why did he have to bring up Greg Maxwell?

"He had a good reason."

"I doubt that." Bing looked earnest. Ellery suddenly caught the same chill thoughts of Greg always brought on.

"Maybe we should go order our dinner." Ellery pulled open the slider and the hot air of the room billowed out. "The waitress is back to get our orders."

At the table, Bing ordered prime rib, and Ellery asked for the same, with a side of slaw. A basket of fresh bread and muffins steamed between them, flanked by little gold-foil packets of butter pats. Ellery reached for a slice and slathered three pats of butter on it. Comfort food was her centering friend.

Bing didn't take any bread. He just gazed across the table at her. It wasn't pity, thank goodness, in his look—more concern. "I'm guessing there's more to the story you told me about the non-wedding. Greg, was that his name?"

Greg. Yes. High school sweetheart. The only man Ellery had ever loved. "While I was first working in Reedsville, at the accounting firm, Greg married someone else. Lisa. She was older than we were in school, popular, wealthy parents. Yes, it crushed me." Like an old tin can, crunching under the steel-posted heel of a boot.

"I thought you said ..."

"After a year or so, they split up, and Greg reached out. He said he wanted us to try, that we hadn't really given us a try."

"So you came back."

"And tried." Ellery looked down at her left hand's ring finger. Empty, where it had once worn a diamond. "I should have known it was too good to be true. For me."

"Don't say that."

Bing was right. She shouldn't say that. She'd spent long, introspective months changing that narrative with herself. She liked herself again until she went mental-tripping back to that rejection.

"While I was fretting about wedding plans—things like whom would I get to walk me down the aisle, since my dad wasn't going to, and Grandpa Bell had just died—Greg only showed passive interest. *Grooms,* I thought at the time. *They never want to make these decisions.* So, I spent nights, my savings, arranging everything from clothes, to the priest, to the venue, to the caterer and the florist, everything. But it turned out Greg wasn't simply apathetic."

Ellery had to stop telling her story while the waitress put the plates of prime rib in front of them. She took a bite of bread to muscle down her heart where it had lodged in her throat.

It didn't work.

"Go on." Bing didn't lift a fork or knife. He didn't even take a sip of water—as if he was too wrapped up in her story.

A story she'd never told anyone. Not Kit. Certainly not Mom. It was too acidic. Too humiliating.

But it looks like I'm going to tell this man who loves God's creatures with reckless abandon and has a giving heart.

"He wasn't apathetic—at least not to someone else." The breadcrumbs turned dry against her tongue. "While I was out wedding shopping, he was ex-wife-visiting. On the morning of our nuptials, Lisa called him to tell him they were expecting a baby."

The tips of Ellery's ears burned—the same temperature as her face afire. She stared at her baked potato, at its sour cream island, at the crinkles of foil where a knife-slice had cut it open.

I wasn't enough for Greg. Twice.

"Ellery." Bing's tender voice cut through the buzzing in her ears and penetrated her dark self-loathing. "I can't even imagine how you felt, losing what you thought was your life's happiness."

Ellery looked up at him, staring, scanning his face. Bing had pinpointed it exactly. It wasn't so much losing Greg himself, as it was losing the vision of where she'd expected her life would go.

"I wanted marriage, kids, to be a family together." Motherhood of more than one child, with a stable father in the home. "His infidelity stole that from me. For a long time it made me think I'd never be enough to make someone choose me first." Her voice cracked, and she had to swallow hard.

Bing's hand shot across the table and grasped hers. His feet reached out as well, hooking his ankles with hers beneath the tabletop, anchoring her to him. "If I ever meet that guy, two things—first, I'll probably punch him in the jaw for treating you so badly. That guy was a jackwagon."

"No, Bing. He's punished enough simply by the fact he has to keep himself company for … forever."

"And second"—Bing went on as if she hadn't interjected—"I'll shake the guy's hand and thank him for showing his true colors *before* he took his vows with you. Because he freed you so that I could meet you."

So Bing could meet her? Did she mean something to him? Was it more than just the crescendo of physical chemistry that had palpably grown between them that kept him around so much? More than the kiss they'd shared on the deck?

No. It couldn't be that he was interested in Ellery. Not truly. He was a tourist in Wilder River, in Ellery's life. He would come in, hear her story, add it to his collection, and move on with his travels.

"I don't blame him anymore. The heart wants what the heart wants. And Greg wanted Lisa."

Bing hadn't let go of her hands, hadn't started on his delicious dinner. "What does your heart want, Ellery?" His eyes were such a deep brown, and the light of the candle flickered in them. "You deserve whatever that is."

In the strength of his gaze, she searched her soul. What did her heart want? Her lips and the rest of her physical body wanted more of Bing, lots more of him. But what did her inner self want?

"Security, I guess." Emotional, financial, spiritual. A safe future. It was something she'd never truly experienced. "Though, that might just be the standard female nature."

Slowly, Bing nodded. Then he let go of her hands, untangled his ankles and stood. He came to her side of the table and lifted her to her feet, and curling his finger to lift her chin, kissed her.

This kiss wasn't sparkling tunnels of ecstasy, it was rocking chairs on a porch in the springtime. It was fresh-baked cookies in the oven. It was laughter with children on a fishing trip to a pond. It was scary and wonderful and fascinating. It was a picture of how security might feel if Bing offered it to her long term.

He broke the kiss and said in a low voice, "You're a revelation, Ellery Hart."

***

The next afternoon, Ellery couldn't get her shirt collar to stay straight—much like her thoughts. A half dozen applicants were coming in to be interviewed for the hostler's job, and she needed her wits. Naturally, her wits had taken a vacation to Optimus Prime Rib, and they were busy gazing out at the cable lights on the pink-stained snow of the ski slopes.

Revisiting Bing Whitmore's kiss. Over and over.

She'd spent the morning getting all arrangements made for Donner and Blitzen's boarding. The pasture out back would be great in the spring, but for now, they needed someplace sheltered. Fortunately, a half block down the road, behind the apple cider press house, was an old horse barn owned by a neighbor who was happy to rent it to Ellery—and he knew a guy selling bales of alfalfa hay.

Stop-gap measures complete! But the sooner she could hire a hostler the better.

"Is it just me, or does Ellery seem off-balance?" Kit and Mom came into the lobby with armloads of Kit's sewing creations. The couch's upholstery looked great against the throw pillows they placed on either edge. "I think she might be twitterpated."

"Guys, I can hear you. I'm right here."

"But are you *here* here, or somewhere over the rainbow?"

"She's dreaming of a white Christmas."

Was she really that obviously discombobulated? "I'm getting ready for my interviews."

"Is that why your shirt is on inside out, and you keep eating your mom's pumpkin cookies out of the cake dome on the counter? The ones for the guests?"

Inside out! "I happen to like pumpkin cookies."

Mom lifted a brow. "I can see that. They're all gone."

All gone! Oh, dear.

"So is half the pot of tea."

Oh, heavens.

Mom put the back of her hand to her mouth and snickered. "It's fine, dear. Now at least I know they're good. You're a discerning eater. Well, maybe not today." Mom came and hugged her. "It's okay, sweetheart. I was in love once, too."

In love! Was that what this was? No. "I'm just nervous about the interviews. They start as soon as the first candidate arrives. We've got to have someone for the horses."

No sign of Bing yet, but there were ten minutes to go. He and Freya had been gone all morning, which she'd expected, but he was supposed to be back to help with the interviews by now.

Headlights appeared down in the drive. The first guy to interview soon came up the steps. Eager, early, excellent. This might be the guy for Donner and Blitzen. He wore a brown barn coat and a leer. "Miz Hart?"

"This way," she said, leading him into the restaurant area and settling him at the table. "Where are you from, Mr. ..."

"Greevis." He spelled it out for her, though she'd seen it in his application.

Oh, that name didn't bode well. Sounded more like *grievous*. "Another interviewer will be here shortly, but we can get started on a few preliminaries."

"That's fine by me, just the two of us." Mr. Greevis's leer roved up and down Ellery's frame.

That had to be because her shirt was on backwards. Nothing more, right?

Shudder.

"What's your experience with horses?" That was what Bing had suggested she ask to start. "Anything recent?"

Mr. Greevis leaned back in his chair and stretched his legs out. "I ride. I bet you do, too. Well. You've got a *nice* seat."

The interview ended quickly. Ellery marched back out into the waiting room, excusing Mr. Greevis with a, *Thanks for applying. I don't think you'll be a good fit for the position,* after which Greevis dropped a truly lewd comment.

Who knew interviewing could be so akin to harassment?

A second guy rolled up in the parking lot outside—just as Bing descended the stairs. He looked even more handsome than ever, his face covered with invisible trails of last night's kisses, even if he was late.

"Sorry. As soon as Freya and I came back from the cocoa shop, I saw you walk in with that first guy, and came right back down as soon as I dropped off my coat. Is he gone already? That was quick."

"Not quick enough." She stretched her neck and shoulders to slough off the residue of greasy Greevis. "I saw down in the parking lot that the second applicant just arrived, though. Let's hope he's less lecherous than the last guy."

"Lecherous!" Bing shout-whispered, since the new guy was entering the lobby.

"Hello," Ellery reached out to shake hands with a man in a yellow stocking cap. "Thank you for coming in."

Yellow Stocking Cap guy had only ever ridden horses at dude ranches. He had never even saddled one on his own. Nope. See ya.

Next, White Stetson guy knew about horses, but when they took him down to the barn behind the cider house to meet Donner and Blitzen, the chemistry between man and beasts was just wrong. Even Ellery could see that.

The final applicant came through the doors, and she was a vision. "Hi, I'm Mattie Jane Daines."

"Hi. So nice to meet you. Would you come in and sit down?" Ellery invited the pretty redhead with the high ponytail and the bright smile to follow her back into the restaurant.

She looked wary, but who wouldn't be during a job interview?

"I'm Ellery Hart, owner of the hotel. This is Bing Whitmore, my …" Boyfriend? "Consultant." Under the table, he placed a hand on her thigh. She covered it with her hand. How could someone be so comforting and discomforting at the exact same time? "Can we start with a little background? What's your experience?"

Mattie looked between the two of them, something between fear and confusion on her face. Finally, she nodded and shrugged. "Well, I have done bicycle tours of downtown Vancouver. I have an excellent sense of direction."

Bicycle tours? Well, at least that showed she might be able to be a great tour guide of Wilder River. Ellery hadn't gotten that far with any of the past candidates for the job. "That's great. Anything else?"

"I'm working on getting my pilot's license, but that's just slowly, piece by piece. I'm best with backcountry. I like hiking, rock climbing, plant identification."

Bing cleared his throat. "What about experience with horses?"

"Uh, some. I like them, if that's what you're asking."

Donner and Blitzen would probably like Mattie. She had a good vibe, but good vibes didn't hook up teams to carriages.

"I'm sorry. I'm a little lost here," the girl said. "Do you always background-check your guests at this hotel? Because if so, that's awesome, and I can send you credentials. I like a place that is very selective."

Guest? At the hotel? Ellery's throat started to sputter. "Oh, my goodness!" She shot to her feet. "You aren't here for the hostler job."

"I'm here for a job, but not with horses. I'm spending the winter in Wilder River as a backcountry guide. Ice climbing, believe it or not. I saw this darling hotel's website and couldn't resist booking a long-term stay here. Sleigh Bells Chalet? That's just amazing."

A guest. They had a long-term guest—besides Bing and Freya.

"Welcome!" Ellery shook Mattie's hand vigorously. So much for professionalism. She really wasn't cut out for it. "Bing and I are in the process of hiring someone to care for a new team of horses and drive a carriage through Wilder River. Please, forgive me for thinking you were our next interviewee. Your timing was too uncanny. Can I give you a free night's stay as compensation?"

Mattie just laughed. "I think the story I'll tell someday will be compensation enough."

Ellery had Lenny take Mattie's bags to her room, which Kit had booked and not told Ellery. Or if she had told her, Ellery's mind had swept it away, too caught up in reliving the kisses from last night.

Speaking of Bing, he appeared at her side. "The last applicant didn't show, I guess."

No, he hadn't.

"I don't know what I'm going to do." There was no one to care for Donner and Blitzen, and Ellery simply didn't have the know-how. "The team is already here, and I don't even know how much to feed them. A bale of alfalfa a day? Is that about right?"

"A bale a day!" Bing stiffened. "I—" He swallowed hard and closed his eyes. Then he opened them and looked right at Ellery. "I can't believe I'm going to say this."

"Say what? That I'm an idiot for buying horses with zero knowledge of how to care for them? Because you'd be right."

"No, that ..." He bit back what looked like pain, and his eyes squeezed shut. With a sharp intake of breath, he blurted, "I'll do it. I'll take care of them—and I'll manage the carriage rides."

"Bing!" No, no way. She couldn't ask him to do that, not when he was still smarting from the accident that had taken Snow White's life. "You have a life in Massey Falls. You can't exactly abandon that and be a tour guide at a hotel."

"Right now, what are your other options?"

None. She had zero options. "It's way too much to ask."

"I know that. But you didn't ask. I'm offering."

Did that mean he meant to stay? With her?

Chapter 13

Bing

What kind of sickness had infected his brain and made him offer to help Ellery with her latest horse predicament?

Oh, right. The ailment he'd contracted when he first kissed her the night before. Or had he been infected by it before that?

The moment I laid eyes on her.

"I'm the one who steered you toward buying such a quality team of horses." He handed Ellery her coat and scarf from behind the reception desk and led her out into the cold. They walked back down toward the barn where the team was stabled. "I have a really good feeling about Donner and Blitzen, and I can't stand by and let any old out-of-work person be in charge of their welfare."

Even though putting himself in charge of their welfare was crazy, considering his penchant for traumatized reactions around equines. *It won't happen with Donner and Blitzen. They know you already,* that little inner voice whispered.

Bing would have slapped the voice if he could have.

"But if you stay, what about your job? I mean, I can't afford to pay you very much. Certainly not the salary you were making at home."

Oh, she didn't need to worry about that. "I couldn't charge you for my work."

"Bing! That's unthinkable! I have to pay you something, I mean—you're an expert. Lifelong experience makes you so valuable."

"Which also means you couldn't afford me." The truth cut through the winter air. "Ellery." He stopped just outside the barn doors. "I wouldn't offer if some part of me didn't know I needed this."

She looked up at him, her dark eyes tender. A few snow crystals accumulated on her lashes and the apple of her cheek. "Thank you," she said at last. "I shouldn't say this, probably, but—I really want you to stay."

Her lower lip trembled, begging to be kissed. With a step toward her on the crunch of snow, he placed a tender kiss on that full mouth, drinking in the cherry sweetness.

But on a dime, that sweetness turned—to spice. Passion flared, with a hiss and pop, like a lit firecracker he still held in his hand. She emitted a soft moan, igniting a conflagration in him. All this latent, hidden, explosive desire within her, and it had been lying in wait, just for him. She was blowing his mind, tearing him apart, and putting him back together, over and over with her kiss.

He might never be able to go back to Massey Falls. At least not ever back to life before he'd kissed Ellery Hart.

Chapter 14

Ellery

Grand opening day! Ellery clasped her hands together and shook her head back and forth to make her tiny bell earrings jingle in her ears. Kit had booked the hotel more than half-full of customers based on all of Ellery's advertising, and they'd rustled up a full slate of bookings for the carriage rides on beyond January. Mattie Jane Daines had even called friends up in Vancouver and talked up the Sleigh Bells Chalet to them.

This might actually be happening. It was like Christmas morning— a few days early.

Kit and Lenny and Mom all wore festive sweaters, and Mom sported a headband with felt reindeer antlers. Not professional—but cute. And it was the Christmas season. What kind of Grinch would tell a woman of a certain age to act appropriately during the holidays?

"All we need is a star on top of the tree," Ellery said. The lobby had been transformed, from dark purple, and bad pastels, and cactuses to bright whites, rich wood tones, and holiday cheer. "Where did you get all the lights and tree decorations, Kit?"

"The decorations I just found on hand." Kit rolled her eyes. "Hoarder mom, remember?"

Oh, right. The fabric had originated as part of Kit's mom's stash, too. "That was so nice of her to share."

"Yeah, but I'm afraid it will throw gasoline on the flames of her obsession. Now she has the excuse to save even *more* junk because her suspicion that *someday someone is going to need this* has been fully confirmed."

"Still, she's very generous." Ellery hugged Kit. "Please, help me thank her somehow."

"If you'll let her ride in the carriage once the initial rush of bookings dies down, she'll die a happy woman. Not that I want her to die—I didn't mean that."

Lenny chuckled. "I was the one who got the lights, Miss Ellery. They were all out in my caretaker's quarters. Don't know why, but they was there, so I thought you could use them. Did you see I put them on the front of the hotel, too?"

"They're perfect, Lenny."

Lenny blushed. "I like my job here. I'm glad you saved the Bells Chalet by turning it into the Sleigh Bells Chalet, Miss Ellery. I hope I get to work here forever."

"Me, too, Lenny."

A pang of worry lanced through Ellery. She'd been so busy with remodeling, horse stuff, and falling into deep love with Bing Whitmore, that she hadn't let concerns about the balloon payment due at Allard Allman's bank even flit through her mind for days and days.

Would these carriage and hotel room bookings be enough to stave off the twin wolves of Allard Allman and his loan-payment deadline?

Footfalls on the newly stained hardwoods of the stairs wrested her attention. Bing wore not only a large grin—the broadest she'd ever seen on his so-handsome face—but also a Dickensian greatcoat and top hat.

"Credit goes to the costume shop on Main Street."

"All you lack is holly and ivy on your hat brim." Ellery snagged some off the newly refinished front desk. "And this." She placed a kiss on his cheek. He smelled like aftershave and mint.

"I lack a *lot* of that, I tell you."

"See?" Mom said. "I told you she was dating a great guy. Only a truly great guy would sacrifice his dignity like that for a woman."

"Mom!" Ellery whirled around. "I think he looks amazing." And smelled even better than that. He could take her on a sleigh ride anytime.

"Oh, I'm just teasing. He looks mighty handsome. Who is the first one to ride in the carriage?" Mom clapped her hands. "Can it be me?"

"Mom!"

Bing took Ellery's hand, lacing his fingers through hers. "The first scheduled carriage ride is at two, but could I possibly take Freya on a test run?"

Oh. Not Ellery? Somehow she'd expected to be out there with him for the maiden voyage.

"Sure."

"I mean, I'd love to have you along. Can you sit up top with me? It's just that Freya met someone here in Wilder River, and she is trying to impress him, it seems. She promised him without asking me first."

Freya had met someone! No way. What a relief, actually, since Ellery had been monopolizing all of Freya's vacation-buddy's time.

"Then again, I'd like to at least give it a real practice run before I even put weight in the carriage. Would you like to come, Ellery?"

"I'd love to."

Chapter 15

Bing

Working with Donner and Blitzen, something had cracked open inside Bing, like the loud clap of a glacier at the earliest thaw of spring.

At first touch of the curry comb, at first clink of the metal on the harnesses, at first graze of the velvet mouth as he put in the bits that would guide the team, he'd bristled.

But at second touch, clink, and graze, Bing's bristling had abated. Eventually, he'd been able to breathe, and then relax completely.

In and out, he inhaled and exhaled the rich, equine scent.

Donner and Blitzen. *Thank you.* He patted their noses and fed them each a handful of oats. *Thank you, Ellery, for the chance to love again.*

Outside in the snappy-cold air of the Sleigh Bells Chalet's grand reopening day, Bing hooked together the harness that would yoke the lovely pair as one. Gently, he led them out of the shed where he'd yoked them and attached them to the carriage, the metal clinking and the sleigh bells on their flanks all a-jingle. What a handsome team, gleaming and ebony in the winter sunlight.

The pip-crack inside him split wide open. He loved these creatures—for their grace and strength and indomitable spirits. In Donner and Blitzen, Bing sensed what he'd felt time and again with the horses he'd worked with at Whitmore Stables: the drive to please, the willingness to work to the edge of capacity, the urge to work.

I love this shining example of God's creations.

He patted Donner's neck, and Donner nuzzled his shoulder.

Bing might have been ready to leave racing behind, but he couldn't imagine a life without horses in it.

As he came to that decision, both a light and a peace suffused his soul. Bing knew it was right.

And yet, a far weightier subject loomed: would Donner and Blitzen be the horses that he worked with next? Because—would their owner have a presence in his life?

"Are we ready?" Ellery walked up to him, wearing white, fur-topped boots, a red sweater and a white vest jacket over it. She looked amazing, especially with her eyes sparkling. "They're incredible! Oh, Bing. I can't imagine anything prettier than this sight."

Not Bing. It would only get prettier when he placed her in the scene.

"Can I give you a hand up?" He lifted her onto the buckboard, and then climbed up beside her. She smelled like Christmas—cherry candle wax and sugar cookies. "Freya and Chip are going to meet us in front of the hotel." He clicked and lightly snapped the reins. Donner and Blitzen stepped in sync, and the carriage shuddered into motion.

Ellery clung to his arm as it bounced over the uneven yard. "I'll need to hang onto you."

And that little whisper-voice wasn't whispering inside him anymore. It was at full shout-volume and saying, Bing would need to hang onto her.

***

"Turns out, your carriage rides through Wilder River were the best advertising I could have done." Ellery's face glowed as she greeted him at the barn where Bing was unhitching the team.

"Yeah?" he asked as he removed the bit from Donner's mouth.

"Yep. With the Sleigh Bells Chalet logo painted on the back of the carriage—thanks to Kit—I've already booked over a dozen rides for the next few days—with people who aren't even staying at my hotel. They said they want to stay with us next time they come to town. Can you believe it?"

"Easily."

Ellery had done it all. She'd saved her grandfather's hotel with her ingenuity and hard work. And her indomitable spirit, just like Rose Red and Snow White had.

"Are the horses going to be up for that?"

"They're draft horses, made for work, and these two seemed happier as the day went on. You could book two dozen rides a day and they'd be in heaven." And he loved them for it.

Ellery sighed in relief. "Oh, good. Because if this keeps up, Donner and Blitzen will have paid for themselves in no time."

"That's fantastic."

"How did your other rides go?" She helped Bing with the breakdown of the tack, hanging it in all its designated places on the wall. "I heard you gave them fake history on the tour and they couldn't stop laughing."

"I learned from the best." Seven carriage rides had filled his afternoon and evening. "Most people I just took touring. Only a few got the fictional Wilder River treatment. But really, it was easy. Fun."

"Just like being with you." Ellery shot him a wink, one that penetrated the thick, callused layers he'd built up.

"Let's take Donner and Blitzen down to their stables." He handed her the reins on Donner's bit. "They deserve a rest." Maybe he'd sneak them an apple for their efforts.

"So do you. Would you like to spend the evening with me?"

Would he! "Are you sure you're not too wiped out?"

"Running a hotel is definitely a wiper-outer, but I'm not feeling it today for some reason." Her boots crunched down the snowy lane in sync with his—just like her horse team when it was in harness. "Without you, Bing, none of this would have happened. I wouldn't have

93

any of the hope that is floating me across the snow right now."

Before he could stop the jumble of thoughts or filter the words, he was talking, too. "You've given me a floating hope, too, Ellery."

"Me?"

He figured he should explain all the reasons why—and tell her the impact she'd had on him. Ringing sounded in his ears, the rush of the blood and the hollering of the feelings inside him, screaming at him to let her know how he was starting to feel every time he woke up in the morning, every time he went to bed at night. That Ellery Hart was his only thought and his only wish, and—

"Hey, Bing?" Ellery said, interrupting his reverie. "Is that your phone? Are you going to get that?"

"Oh, huh? What?" Sure enough, it wasn't a ringing in his ears—well, it was. Only a literal ringing. "Hello?" He handed Ellery the reins to Blitzen as well, just as they approached the doors to the barn where the horses were being boarded. "This is Bing Whitmore."

He hadn't bothered to check the number, but he knew the voice on the other end instantly. "Bing? I hate to interrupt your vacation. Freya told me not to—under any circumstances. But I thought you'd want to know this. Please don't fire me."

"It's all right, Reggie." They guy taking care of Whitmore Stables in Bing's absence had Bing's full confidence. "What's going on?"

Heat sizzled from Bing's toes up to the roots of his hair. This couldn't be good. The air crackled with *not good*.

Reggie cleared his throat, and Bing could almost picture him wincing. "It's Rose Red."

"What about her?" Bing's voice was thin, a single thread. "She's not—"

"She's still with us, but she doesn't look good. Dr. Harrison thinks it's an infection. He brought in Dr. Wilson for a second opinion."

"And?" It came out almost as a whisper.

"And they both think you should come home."

Now the ringing in Bing's ears commenced for real. It silenced everything else, except the throbbing of his heart in his throat. He stood a long time.

"Bing?" Reggie broke through.

"I'm … I'll be there. Keep her going for me until I get there."

Chapter 16

Ellery

"Week two and wouldn't you say we're managing fine?" Kit said, her voice unsure, but fake-reassuring at the same time. "I mean, with that Reggie guy who dropped in out of nowhere, it's not like we don't have anyone to run the horse and carriage business. The hotel is full."

"And I keep getting compliments on my clove- and nutmeg-blend tea." Mom shoved more than half a sugar cookie in her mouth at once. "Mmm. These cookies. They're so moist."

Even with the apple cinnamon candle warmer melting on the desktop filling every inhaled breath, and with Kit's tree trimmed to a heart-stopping degree and filling half the lobby, and even with nearly every room in the hotel filled with ski-toting guests—Ellery couldn't feel anything but a vast chasm.

If anyone were to whisper in her ear, or pat her on the back, the echo could have deafened all of Wilder River.

"The beverages and baked goods are great, Mom."

Kit tugged on Ellery's arm. "Come with me." She took the ledger, shut it, and stuffed it beneath the counter. "Enough tea. You need some serious chocolate. A lot of it. And hot."

There wasn't enough hot chocolate in the entire world to fill the emptiness.

Ellery followed Kit through the french doors into the yet-to-be-reinstated hotel restaurant. Kit sat her down, and a minute later brought two mugs of steaming cocoa. "I know you hate the marshmallows, so I left them out."

Steam floated, but it didn't blur her vision any more than it already was. "Thanks." Her voice was flat. Two-dimensionality had overtaken her world.

Kit took a sip, but pulled the cup away quickly. "Ouch."

"Are you okay?"

"Yes"—Kit smirked—"but you're not."

Gah! No kidding! "I'm fine. It's Christmas. The hotel's coming back. You said so yourself."

"Your Grandpa Bell would be so proud of the way you've turned the place around."

"Yeah." Ellery pushed her mug a little, and a ripple skated across the chocolaty surface. "He loved this place."

Kit exhaled heavily. "Ellery."

Ellery didn't lift her eyes. The ripples in the cup softened and died. "You don't have to say it. I know what's coming."

"Yes, Bing Whitmore left."

Just as Ellery had predicted. A salt shaker for her wound. "He was a guest. That's what guests do. They check in, and then they check out." Seven long days had passed since Bing Whitmore checked out, and nothing had come from him, other than his friend Reggie.

"But sometimes they check into your heart but not out of it."

"Please pass the crackers to go with all that cheese." Why did Kit have to keep stating the painfully obvious? "At least he sent a replacement hostler until I can find someone trustworthy for Donner and Blitzen."

"But there's no replacement. Not for him—is there?"

Geez, Kit. Leave it alone! It wasn't like Ellery had any control over Bing's decision to leave, and she wouldn't have asked him to stay anyway. He had a sick horse, one that was extremely important to him.

He'd been up front with her on that topic. Rose Red mattered to him immensely.

"In a warped way, it's kind of a pattern." Ellery traced the floral design on the tablecloth. "Men show an interest in me, and then they remember their greater interest lies somewhere else."

"If you're saying you're not enough—just stop. Ellery Hart, stop this very second."

Stop what? Falling head over heels for Bing Whitmore? Stop hurting that he left? That he chose another over her? Stop wishing she hadn't let herself open up to him so much that he'd climbed right inside and made a stall inside her heart, that she'd strawed just for him?

"He will come back."

He wouldn't. He had enormous responsibility in a town nine hours' drive from where Ellery had her own list of enormous responsibilities. His grandfather's stable, her grandfather's hotel. Geography didn't just fold itself to bring distances like that closer.

"I'll be fine either way." Sort of. Eventually, just like she was fine a couple of years down the road from Greg's rejection. Except—this had felt so much more real than it ever had with Greg. Bing filled the empty little places inside her that she'd never even noticed were there.

Which was probably why his going away was such a scooping out of her inner self.

"Ellery, he's really into you. I just know he will come back." Kit pulled out her phone. "Let's just look him up online. He's kind of well-known." She tapped the screen while Ellery folded in on herself. "See? Look. Bing Whitmore." She held up the screen for Ellery to see. "Owner of Snow White, owner of Rose Red, dating female jockey—"

Smooth. Really smooth, Kit. "See? He won't come back."

"No, Ellery! This is old news. Top female jockey Shayla Sharp and thoroughbred stables owner Bing Whitmore ..." Kit started mumbling as she scrolled the article.

This wasn't helping. "Thank you for the cocoa." She slid back, her knee bumping the table's leg and sloshing brown liquid over the rim and onto the white cloth, making a stain spread as the liquid wicked outward. "I'll wash that. Don't worry."

"You didn't even have a sip." Kit scrambled to her feet. "And this isn't something to worry about, Ellery."

She hadn't been—until Kit brought it up.

Why did it smell like Mom was burning an empty teapot on a stove somewhere nearby?

Lenny flew through the french doors. "Ellery! There you are." He was breathing hard. "I was looking everywhere."

"What's wrong?" Any other problem would have been preferable to talking about Bing's abandonment. "Is someone at the front desk? I'll come right away."

"Good! But it's not a guest." Lenny strode beside her. "It's that banker. Allard Allman."

Ellery took it back. *Almost* any other problem would be preferable. "Did he say what he wanted?"

"He says your payment is due right this second."

***

"Miss Hart." Allard Allman's eyes sat too close together. His fingernails were dirty from all the coins he counted in his counting house all day. He probably had a blood type that predisposed him to greed, too. "Thank you for accompanying me on this sleigh ride."

"You booked it for the rest of the afternoon, but we do need to be considerate of the horses." Ellery shot a glance at Reggie in the carriage-driver's seat. Maybe he'd catch the hint and shorten this joyride. Er, *joyless* ride. "You said you wanted to talk business with me?"

"Business, yes." Allard slid closer on the tufted seat, his shoulder bumping Ellery's. "But it doesn't have to be all business. It could evolve."

Uh, no. It could not. "I realize that my loan is due. I have partial payment available now, and the promise of the remainder by the end of January. We have plenty of bookings."

"Partial?"

"Yes." She detailed the amounts she could scrape together, if she didn't pay herself back for the money she'd invested in Donner and Blitzen from the last of her personal savings account. "It's not all there now, but it will be. I guarantee it."

"Your signature on the loan agreement should have been the guarantee, you know."

True. True enough. "Eighteen months ago, I was operating under the full expectation that the hotel would bounce back into solvency within six months. It has taken longer, but now we definitely have a game plan and are seeing astounding results. I'm sure you noticed the remodeling work in the lobby—as well as the rebranding we did."

"All on the bank's dime."

No, none of it on the bank's dime. Not directly. "I had a lot of volunteer workers, as well as donations. Everyone pulled together to save the hotel—because everyone loved my grandpa."

Allard Allman's breath steamed, and it smelled like sausages and gravy. "I think you know that a contract is a contract. It's binding."

"I do, but—" Why was he being difficult? "Doesn't the bank want its money? I can let you see all the hotel's financials from the past couple of weeks. There's no doubt in my mind you'll see that your investment will be returned."

"Investment? It was a loan."

Weren't they the same thing, when it came to banks? "Please, Mr. Allman."

"Call me Allard." He turned an oily leer on her and ran a dry, bumpy, lizard-like tongue across his upper lip. "I do see a possible way around this difficulty, Miss Hart, if you're willing to think creatively."

Oh, no. No-no-no-no-no. "Mr. Allard, I'd like to discuss extending my loan's due date by several weeks, if possible, based on solid expectations."

"If they're expectations that align with my own, we can definitely talk." Allard sniffed. "How does this sound, Ellery? I'd be honored to call you Ellery, rather than Miss Hart."

Miss Hart would continue to be fine. "If you need to ratchet up the interest rate for the final weeks, I can see the business purpose in that."

"These will not be monetary negotiations, Ellery." The way he said her name sent ants crawling up her neck. He slid his arm around her shoulders. "I've noticed you for years. Even when you were dumped so unceremoniously by that pinhead Greg Maxwell, I was keeping an eye on you."

Stalker much? "Mr. Allman—"

He didn't let her interrupt. "I bided my time, waiting until you were sure to be healed from that humiliation, and now I'm ready to strike a bargain with you. It will be mutually beneficial, I have no doubt."

The back of Ellery's throat collapsed, and she had to swallow to force it open. She was already flush against the side of the carriage, and there was no way to scoot farther away from his tentacles. "Mr. Allman!"

"With a few minor concessions on your part—that I'll detail in private"—he shot a look at Reggie—"the loan can be forgiven. In its *entirety*. The hotel will be yours, free and clear."

She clenched her teeth. "And if not?"

"Then I begin foreclosure proceedings. As soon as the court deems, the Sleigh Bells Chalet, your grandfather's legacy, will belong to the bank."

"But what about the staff?" Where would Kit go? And Lenny? Mom! She'd practically grown up at the Bells Chalet.

"That will be up to the new owner, of course. Your staff will be let go just in time for Christmas. I'm sure you're beginning to see things my way. My way is a good way, Ellery, for you—and for me." He leaned his face into hers, his hot breath brushing her cheek.

The carriage jerked wildly to the right, throwing Allard Allman away from Ellery, who was gripping the side of the carriage.

"Stop the horses," she called. "I need to get out." She leaped from the door, swinging it shut and leaving Mr. Allman and his unpleasant suggestions on the pretty upholstery.

"Sleep on it, Ellery. Dream of me. I'm sure you'll see things my way by morning. I'll be in touch."

Chapter 17

Bing

Massey Falls was blanketed in snow, and more was coming down. The Whitmore Stables stable hands were up on the roofs shoveling the two feet of white stuff away to the ground to prevent collapse. The sounds of the world were muffled, even the whinnies and grunts from the stables.

But Rose Red's voice was forever muffled.

And Bing was completely done.

"It's not just a horse to you. I know that." Dr. Harrison put an arm around Bing's shoulders. "They're never just a horse. People who haven't loved them won't understand."

Bing couldn't feel his face, and it wasn't just from the cold.

"You really loved her," Freya said. "We all did, but you most of all."

"I wish the surgery could have prolonged her life more." Dr. Wilson's voice sounded strangled. He'd been the surgeon, in the long shot procedure a few weeks ago. "If I'd had an operating table, or better setting skills ..." His voice got a little strangled. "I'm so sorry."

The illness wasn't a complication of the surgery. It just ... was.

"It's not your fault." It wasn't anyone's fault. Horses died. That was the lesson to be taken from this. Loved ones left this life. Abandoned the living. "I appreciate what you all did to try to save her over the past week. Pneumonia is no joke."

Bing's own lungs were filling up with fluid. His heart was sloshing in it, and drawing breath grew more and more difficult.

"Let's get you inside," Freya said. "You're shaking."

Shaking? Yeah, he was shaking, all right. He was more than shaking—he was shaken. He stumped toward the house on the far side of the stable grounds, the place he'd spent the past eight years of his life—since Grandpa Whitmore passed away and the running of the thoroughbred operation became Bing's full time world.

The door of the house opened and a wall of heat came at him, but it wouldn't penetrate him. Not for a long time.

Freya pulled out a painted-white wooden armchair for him at the kitchen table. He sat down, and its spindles ground against his back, even through his parka.

"Maybe we can see if the Torrey Stakes Racetrack will let Snow White and Rose Red share a burial site."

Rose Red hadn't even run in the local stakes. Not once. She'd fallen even before her debut run. "Who of the cousins do you think would buy me out?"

Freya dragged a chair across the tile and sat down beside him. "We're back to that discussion, are we?"

"It's not even that, actually. It's not about Rose Red, or Snow White. Not anymore." The idea solidified in his head as he spoke the words. "It's been a while since my heart was in racing."

"You love the horses, but not the business." Freya picked up a salt shaker from the middle of the table and set it back down. "I think I get it. That's what you were trying to say before."

Whether he'd known it or not. Yeah.

"As a trained professional, I should have listened better. Sorry, Bing."

"I don't want to close Whitmore Stables, not if someone else wants to run it."

Slowly, Freya nodded. "The things you did for the business—it won't be easy to replace your work. Your devotion."

Plenty of guys loved horses. That shouldn't be a problem. "But you're saying the family might eventually understand that I need out?"

She set her phone on the table. "There's been a cousin group text."

"I didn't get any texts."

"You were excluded from these. Sorry."

So the thread was about him. "Some kind of intervention plot?" Got it. "They all think I'm wimping out."

"They all think you're as big of a champion as Snow White ever could have been for keeping Grandpa's dream alive this long. No one else is ready to step up to the plate. They all are like me. They have lives. Families that need their attention."

The horses and stable hands had been Bing's life and family, absorbing all his attention and time. "Unlike me."

"Yet, Bing. You haven't got that yet." She tipped back and balanced on her chair. "Remember that word? You've used it before."

He exhaled heavily. Hope didn't float, it fled—in his universe.

"Actually, even I think I'd like to make a life-changing move. Follow your lead and get away from the constant pressure of clients' needs and start thinking about making a difference in a more personal manner."

Was she talking about moving, literally? As in, to Wilder River? "You really like that school teacher, don't you?"

"Let's just say that our vacation may have shifted the trajectory of more than one life."

For real? She met a guy tending the bar in a hot cocoa shop, and— "Well, that's great. I knew you were spending time with him, but I hadn't realized it was serious."

"It's getting there. Which means, I'm not exactly the top candidate for taking over Whitmore Stables and the day-to-day running of the business, let alone the horse needs."

"There's no one in the family who can step up to the plate." Bing was in a trap, and the clamp of its metal jaws gouged into his limb, keeping him captive. "I need to sell, but there's no one to sell to." Much as he was desperate to walk away, there was no one to make this possible.

Not for him. Bing's head throbbed, in concert with his heart. *Rose Red. I'm so sorry.*

"I'll tell you what was said in the group text." Freya took out her phone, but then pulled it back. "But first, I want to know a few things."

"From me?"

"Yeah. First, what have you lost?"

"You mean besides Snow White and Rose Red? And everyone's investment in them?" And, temporarily, his solid footing? "I mean, yeah. There's more loss. For instance, my drive to do this job."

"Okay, but that was waning before."

Long before. If he were honest, it was waning long before Snow White's accident as well. It might sound not-so-macho of him, but he didn't like seeing the horses pushed to their extremity. He'd rather see a good trail horse bear a rider up a gentle slope to a ridge's vista or a draft team like Donner and Blitzen pull a carriage.

Donner and Blitzen. He'd grown too fond of them in too short a time.

And of their owner.

"Yeah. Waning. To emptiness."

"Let me put on my professional psychologist's hat again, then."

"Not this again." Please. As if he could stop her.

"The word empty has come up several times in the past day— while we traveled back to Massey Falls, and over and over since then. It's a theme, if I'm right."

She wasn't wrong.

"I take it from your silence you agree. So, tell me, Bing. What would fill you?"

Besides getting away from this soul-sucking responsibility of Grandpa's stables and keeping a dream alive that wasn't his own? "I don't know."

"I think you do."

Fine. He knew. "But I left her. While we were on death-watch for Rose Red, Ellery Hart texted me and wished me good luck in all my endeavors."

"Oh."

"Yeah."

"Them's dumping words."

No kidding. "I left her, even when I knew she'd been left before. Even when I knew that was her Achilles' heel."

Freya almost visibly took off her professional hat. "You are a jerk."

"I know." And now what was done was done, and Ellery wasn't going to trust him ever again. "I guess it bites the most because for a while I'd been telling myself I could be what she needed."

"And what was that?" Freya put all four legs of the chair back on the ground. "Did you know?"

"Actually, yeah. She told me. Explicitly." Which made it easy. "Security."

Again, Freya gave her slow nod. Maybe that was something they trained for in her profession. "Most women do. That's a deep-seated, inherent craving of a woman's soul."

"And I blasted any hope of being a safe place for her to smithereens." Kaboom.

"By coming to check on Rose Red?"

"By not letting her know I choose her first. Over everything else." Which—he had. Or at least he realized it now, even though he had failed to prove it to her. And which he now ached to prove to her. Oh! But why on earth would she trust him now?

Freya sighed. "Sounds to me like you have your work cut out for you."

"Work?"

"Proving that you're a better risk than you seem."

Was it even possible to prove such a thing—especially when he was as broken as he was? "Tell me what the group text said."

And please let it be a way out.

Chapter 18

Ellery

"**J**ust sign on the line, please, Miss Hart."

They were back to formal titles again, thank heavens. But along with those formal titles came the Molotov cocktail to burn down Grandpa Bell's legacy.

"Don't do it, Ellery!" Lenny hollered, bounding through the lobby, toting a huge water jug decorated like a reindeer's head on his shoulder. It clinked and jingled. "I have my savings right here. It's all yours, like I told you. And they's ten more just like this. It'll be more than five thousand dollars, if I'm guessing right."

Oh, Lenny. You have the best heart in a hundred-mile radius.

"Too little too late," Allard Allman chortled. "Though I do admire your friends' devotion to you. I could have been your friend, may I remind you?"

No, he may not.

"Friends don't foreclose on friends," Kit said, shaking her jingle bell necklace at him like a curse from a witch's talisman. "She forked over more than half of the debt to you and was going to have the full amount to you in a month. You couldn't wait that long? I know what you are, Allman, Ebenezer Scrooge himself. The Ghost of Christmas Yet to Come will have you in his sights. Watch out for that scythe, pal."

"Kit!" Ellery signed her legal name on the line. "It's my decision. I

109

borrowed the money, and I was responsible to pay it back. This is a natural consequence to the choices I made."

"Yeah, I gave her a way out. She chose not to take it." Allard's voice dripped with sarcasm. "But now I'm glad—especially since I already have a buyer on the hook for this place."

A buyer! Already? Ellery clutched at her heart. "Oh!" Until that second, it hadn't seemed real. It had seemed like a terrible dream, but one she could wake up from. Or like a movie with alternate endings in the bonus features, one she could rewind and see the other version, the real one, where she didn't lose the hotel, where she didn't squander her grandfather's dream.

"Mr. Allman, you're selling so soon?" she squeaked unintentionally, when she meant to sound confident and bold. "I mean, I was planning on ..."

On what? Convincing a different bank to take *another* wild risk on her and loaning her the money to buy the hotel out of hock from Allard Allman's bank? What crazy lender would consider doing that? Probably no one. She'd proved herself to be an exceptionally bad risk. Not only was Allard Allman taking her property, he was ruining her credit in the process.

"The buyer was very forthcoming. It was a cash offer."

Cash! "As in there won't be a waiting period while the loan is approved?"

"The title can transfer"—he looked at his watch—"within hours, if the new owner simply makes the trip to the bank from where he lives out of town." A smile slithered across his face. "Such a shame. We could have had a beautiful business relationship, you and I. Your loss."

"But—the employees! Are they guaranteed jobs? Lenny lives on the property. He's got nowhere else to go." And what would Mom do? This wasn't just Ellery's legacy—this place had been part of Mom's world for her entire life.

"All things you might have taken into consideration before making your *final* decision." Allard Allman perused the stack of papers, then with a fell swoop, he folded them and stuck them in his pocket. "The keys to the establishment, please."

Oh. So soon? "I'll just …" She dug in her pocket, and then in her purse.

A gong sounded somewhere inside Ellery, lower than a death knell and twice as sinister. It was so stupid. This could have been prevented. Maybe she shouldn't have been so selfish and prideful. Her knees were mere inches from the floor. She could have fallen onto them. Maybe Allard Allman would reconsider if Ellery begged now.

Or not—from the sneer on Allman's face, as if she were a piece of moist, broken candy cane covered with carpet fuzz.

"I'll be leaving now. You were never worth the effort." He slammed the bell-strung door behind him, letting in an icy blast.

Mom, Lenny, and Kit all stared at her. Ellery gripped the newly-topped registration desk to stay vertical.

"It's over?" Kit's voice scratched. "Just like that?" She glanced around at the work she'd accomplished. "I thought, somehow, that what we'd done for this place would be enough."

I thought I would be enough. A hiccupy moan lurched from Ellery's throat. "I'm really, really sorry, everyone. Mom—I let you down. If you want me to, I'll go after him. I'll throw myself on his mercy."

"Hush your mouth!" Mom gathered Ellery in her arms. "Yes, I want you to have a husband, but not that way. And definitely not that one." She blew a raspberry in Allard Allman's general direction. "You're my darling daughter, and he's a bottom-dwelling miscreant. *You*, my dear, are worth ten thousand Sleigh Bells Chalets."

A hot smear of tears squished down Ellery's cheeks, probably consisting of black sludge. She sniffled, and not in a cute, feminine way. She pressed her face into Mom's shoulder, which smelled like pumpkin cookies—which made the whole thing worse, and Ellery erupted in sobs. "I couldn't give myself to him. Not even for this place. I'm so sorry."

Ellery loved these people, and she loved this place—but blast it!—she had a love for herself, too. Even if Greg Maxwell hadn't seen it. Even if Bing Whitmore was blind to it. Ellery possessed value—something intrinsically good inside herself. Something worth cherishing. She couldn't lavish what was precious and sacred—her very soul and her love and her *self*—on anyone who wouldn't prize her.

Especially not on an unappreciative eel like Allard Allman.

Until someone did see her for the precious woman she was, she would have to stand firm, even if she were the only one who saw her inherent value.

"You were right to do that, Ellery." Lenny placed a meaty hand on her head and swished the tips of her hair.

Okay, so Lenny might see her worth, too. And Kit. And Mom. It was great to have people in her life who were okay with her choosing not to sell out to a jerk in order to protect their livelihoods.

Annnnd, she was crying all over again. "I'm sorry, guys. I kind of ruined everybody's Christmas, eh?"

"Who says Christmas is ruined?" Mom asked. "I still have cinnamon-orange tea."

"And I gots lots and lots of money in my change jars." Lenny grinned. He was missing a tooth halfway back on his right uppers. Seeing that broad of a smile made a little sugarplum fairy dance in Ellery's heart. "You know how I told Mr. Allman I had ten more jugs like this? I lied."

Oh, no. So Lenny didn't have a savings to fall back on? Oh, dear. The nose-running started afresh, and Ellery's eyes stung. "Oh, Lenny. I'm—"

"Nope. I gots about fifty more. But I wasn't gonna tell that goat about it. He had 'mean one Mr. Grinch' written all over him, and he mighta come out to the handyman's quarters and said my jugs was on the property and they belongs to him, too. I could see the avarice in the tilt of his eyes."

Avarice in the tilt of his eyes! Good phrase, Lenny. "I'm glad you didn't tell him. And great job saving for your future."

"Oh, that's just what's in my jugs. I gots a few savings accounts, too. Here and there. I'm thinking about making an offer on the Sleigh Bells Chalet, if I can trick Mr. Allman and his bank into not knowing it's an offer coming from me. Somehow's I gotta find out how much the cash buyer was telling him they'd be paying. Then I'll double it!" Lenny let out a laugh worthy of Santa Claus.

"Bless you, Lenny!"

The bell tower of the nearby church struck five. "The bank will be closed until morning, so you sleep on that decision," Ellery said, giving Lenny a hug. "You're the best friends and family any girl ever had." She placed a kiss on her fingertips and pressed them to his cheek.

Lenny beamed. "Anything for you, Ellery."

That? That was love. That was cherishing. Even if Lenny wasn't her match, he knew how to make her feel like she mattered.

She needed that—at least as much as she needed security in life.

In fact, maybe being loved by someone who made her feel that way, who truly believed she deserved it, *was* security.

"From what Allman said, I guess we will have to clear out in the morning." Kit pulled Ellery out the door. "For now, let's go get a holiday meal. I've got leftover turkey and potatoes to warm up. My hoarder mom is a fantastic cook, if you'll recall."

Ellery had a few things to wrap up. For instance, the guests had to be told to pay their bills and plan to check out in the morning. Ellery wouldn't be there. The hotel belonged to someone else.

Allard Allman would have to figure all that out. Maid service, checkout times, guest complaints, the continental breakfast.

Was that what he wanted? Well, he had it. And more power to him.

They locked up on their way out, and Ellery wouldn't have a key to get back in.

It was over.

Chapter 19

Ellery

"Shhh. Shhh." Ellery rubbed down the side of Donner's neck, brushing him with the curry comb just the way she'd seen Bing do it. "That's a good boy. Do you like the oats?"

Reggie had left for his morning coffee. Just as well. Ellery could use some time to talk to the team.

"I guess we're not going to be doing what you were trained to do, after all, boys." She lifted a handful of oats for Blitzen to eat from her palm. The black velvet mouth brushed softly against her skin. They were beautiful animals, both of them. She'd already gotten used to them. "I'm sorry about that."

Maybe she could still put them in harness to finish out the bookings, just not have the team leave from in front of the hotel. But would guests be able to find the stable where Donner and Blitzen were boarded? It could be confusing to have to come the extra two-blocks' walk to find the carriage starting point.

It made a lot more sense to put the team and the carriage up for sale—possibly to the new owner of the Sleigh Bells Chalet.

And just when the new name of the hotel was starting to make sense.

The jingle bells attached to the horses' tails had been so charming.

It hurt to have to see it end.

All of it.

"You boys liked it, too. I could tell." They really were a great team together. "Didn't you? Didn't you? That's right." She rubbed the side of Donner's warm neck, and he huffed a snort of approval.

Good horse. No wonder Bing had been so attached to his horses. Ellery had only been a horse owner for a matter of days, and she already thought of them as part of herself. She was already having full-on, one-sided conversations with them but inventing their responses in her head. How much more must Bing have felt for those colts and fillies he'd seen born, watched grow, ridden, trained, raced, and cared for daily.

And those that he had seen fall.

And die.

Poor Rose Red. Poor Bing. Reggie had told Ellery—Rose Red hadn't made it.

At least the female jockey would understand and be able to comfort Bing in a way that Ellery couldn't have understood—before now.

No wonder he turned to her. Shayla whatever her name was. It made sense. Ellery hadn't ever loved a horse up to now, so she couldn't have been the rock Bing needed in a time of crisis.

I forgive you, Bing. She didn't cry again—all her tears were spent, evaporated in a dry, salty patch on her mother's shirt's shoulder until it went into the laundry. *Because I get it. Finally.*

And she got something else, too: why Greg went back to Lisa. It wasn't because he was an unmitigated jack-wagon—it was because he was a discerning, *mitigated* jack-wagon … to Ellery. While, at the same time, Greg was a stand-up guy to Lisa, whose child he'd fathered.

Greg Maxwell *should* go be the father of his child, and the husband of the child's mother. It was the right thing he'd done.

By them.

If not by Ellery.

And Ellery never had the same stakes in the game that Lisa had

had in that moment. Not even close.

Not to mention the fact that eventually, like it or not, the whole Greg-Lisa-Baby dynamic would have bled into the Greg-Ellery relationship and likely wrecked it in *Titanic* fashion by this point in time, and Ellery wouldn't have had Greg now anyway.

Hindsight, hindsight, hindsight.

Truly, as Bing said, she'd made a narrow escape.

Whew.

Interesting how being with these horses had unlocked all those realizations, bless them. "All the boys in my life for now are you two, right?" She patted Donner, and then Blitzen.

"Uh, Miss Hart?" Reggie swung around the corner and into view.

How long had he been listening? Great.

"Don't worry. Everyone pours out their hearts to their horses. I didn't hear a thing." He winked. Cute kid. "But, hey. There's someone here to see you."

"Please say it's not the new owner of the Sleigh Bells Chalet." Not now. Maybe not ever. "Tell whomever it is I'm fine with letting go of the hotel, but the carriage belongs to my great uncle, and the horses belong to me. They're not transferring ownership, because they're mine." Forever.

A strong footfall clomped over the wooden slats of the stables. "Are you sure you won't share? Not even a little?"

Bing!

Ellery dropped the curry comb, and when she bent to grab it, she came up fast, whacking the back of her head against Donner's chin. He whinnied and backed up, his large frame stepping as loudly as Bing's boots on the floor.

"Ouch. Are you all right?"

"It comes full circle, now, doesn't it? I was asking you that question the first time we met."

Why show up now? Probably he was here to fetch Reggie. And with that, maybe he was being magnanimous and making sure she'd either found a new hostler to replace Reggie, or else that she could sell Donner and Blitzen. In which case, she'd thank him and deal with her own responsibility.

"Oh, about my ankle. Right." Bing stepped close, right into her scent bubble. He smelled like leather and aftershave. She blinked those scents away as a defense against their dark arts of weakening her knees. "My ankle is doing much better, thank you. In case you're wondering."

"More like wondering what you're doing here."

"I thought Reggie told you."

"The only person he said was coming was the new owner of the hotel. I assume he's showing up here eventually to take my horses, but he can forget it because I'm here to defend them. I have a curry comb and I'm not afraid to use it." She brandished the comb at the imaginary foe.

"Cool your jets, girl. I have no intention of taking Donner and Blitzen from you."

"You. I'm not talking about you."

"You're talking about the new owner of the hotel."

"Yeah. Exactly."

He raised his eyebrows. Confusion blurred inside her.

"Wait. What's going on? I'm not giving up the horses. I know I can't take care of them, but I'm fully invested, and they were never owned as part of the hotel itself." The carriage rides were her only source of income—for now.

"I can see you're getting attached to them."

Yeah, but ... "But I still don't get why you're here." Bing had gone off to be with his lady-jockey friend, to mourn the passing of his beloved horse. It made no sense for him to come back here.

"Isn't it obvious?"

Uh ... no. Did he just want to taunt Ellery? Or was this an exercise in prolonging the inevitable? He'd come to break up with her in person.

"If you've come back here to tell me you're leaving again, I'd say you made a long drive. But Bing—really. I'm fine." Sort of. If a person with a hollowed-out section of her heart could be termed fine. It'd grow back. Eventually. Probably. Or she'd learn to function without it. "The hotel has been sold, so I'm just figuring out what to do with my life next. I was waiting to see who bought it, and if it's a cool person, I'll try to work out a deal—try to see whether Donner and Blitzen will be helpful to the Sleigh Bells Chalet."

And if not, she'd just go back to being an adult. Sell the horses to someone who would treat them right, go back to Reedsville, and beg for her old accounting job back. It was the grown-up thing to do. It made sense. And it was her next logical move.

While simultaneously ripping her to shreds.

"I was hoping you'd let me in on part of that decision-making process. And let me see these beautiful horses." He really did seem to admire them.

"You came all this way to give me life advice? Isn't that more your cousin Freya's line of work?"

"I'm back because I bought some property here in Wilder River."

He had? This shouldn't have made Ellery's heart go for a world-record high jump because all signs pointed to her leaving soon. But it did set the record, plus it added a flip at the end of the jump.

"Oh?" she fought to keep her tone even. "Where is it? I mean, that's really nice. You'll like it here. Me, I'm heading back to Reedsville. Probably getting my accounting job back. Or some other job crunching the numbers. Working with customers all the time—it's pretty taxing."

"Reedsville? Are you sure?"

No, she wasn't sure. "Where did you say your property was?"

"Up the road a couple of blocks. It's a really good investment. And it has horse property attached, so it was pretty much a no-brainer."

"Horse property? In town?" What kind of place was that? The only in-town lot with a fenced area was … "The Sleigh Bells Chalet?" Her voice was tight, a stretched thread. "You?"

"Reggie told me it was coming on the market. I put in a cash offer the bank couldn't refuse."

He—he—he … "You did?" she breathed. Everything in the stable tilted on its side. Ellery stepped out of the stall and closed the latch.

"Uh-huh." He wore a warm smile, not the villain's twisted-end-mustache-sinister grin she'd expected on the new owner of her grandfather's hotel.

Ellery's mouth was dry. "I don't understand. You have Whitmore Stables, a jockey girlfriend, a family business to run." A life. A far away, a nine-hour-drive-from-here life. "You can't run the Sleigh Bells Chalet from out of town."

"No. You're right."

Did it mean … "You can't be relocating to Wilder River." Not right as Ellery was heading off to Reedsville.

"You don't want me to?"

It wasn't that. It was … "If it's what you want, it's a good place to be. I've learned a lot about myself in this town. It's a healing place. You've been through a lot, so, I mean, I hope you find what you're looking for here." She was babbling.

Bing stepped closer, and Ellery's back went flush against the wall of the stall. He smiled down at her. "I think I already have."

All the babbling died in her throat. He was so near, almost sharing her air.

"And for the record"—his voice was sultry, like he wanted her as much as she was starved for him and his touch and his attention and his love—"there's no jockey girlfriend. Never was."

"But the online article—"

A chortle erupted from a few stalls down. "You need to check the dates on your gossip columns, Miss Ellery." Reggie emerged, looking sheepish and tipping his hat. "Sorry for eavesdropping. I couldn't find a gracious way to leave once you two got started talking. I'll just go now. But please, for the love of Christmastime, kiss that woman, Bing. She's not going to keep forever. And you've done enough delaying as it is."

Reggie swung himself over the stall gate and hustled out into the snowy morning.

"Check the dates?" she asked. "You're not together with Shiloh What's-her-name?" Or was it Shayla?

"Never was."

"Oh." What else should Ellery say? "And you came back—and bought the Sleigh Bells Chalet—because …?"

"Because I fell in love here."

"With the hotel?"

"With a beautiful girl who loves her family enough to give up her career to perpetuate a grandfather's dream." He placed a kiss above her right eye. "Who made me smile again." He placed a second kiss above her left eye. "Who has recently discovered that horses are some of the best listeners." He kissed the tip of her nose. "Reggie did mention …"

"Oh, great. Reggie! He is so fired." Or hired—as a matchmaker. "As punishment I'm going to put that guy on carriage-driver duty on New Year's Eve when everyone is making out with their dates in the carriage, just to keep him awkward all evening long."

"Poetic justice will be served." Bing unbuttoned his jacket and pulled out a folded piece of paper from a pocket inside. "I heard all about how it happened, and about that banker's vendetta. Yeah, from Reggie—again." He held the paper out to her.

"Oh?" Maybe Reggie wouldn't have to drive on New Year's Eve. At least not the late shift. "What's this?" She took the paper he was offering. "The deed to the hotel?" From within it fell a key.

"I put your name back on it when I recorded it this morning downtown at the courthouse. I hope that's okay."

Okay! It was the most generous, incredible thing anyone had ever done for her. How could he afford something like this? "How did you— but, your *life*?"

"My extended family came together, conspired against me. They, uh, fired me, actually, on Doctor Freya Whitmore's orders. They said I needed a change of scenery. For now, my duties will be transferred to a local veterinarian named Harrison who is retiring and just wants to concentrate on horses and his collectibles."

"Someone can do your job?"

"Probably better than I ever did it."

Hard to believe. "But what about you? Are you selling your shares in the business?"

"I'm keeping my interests in the stables, but they gave me a nice severance package for my work there, and I decided to invest it."

"In the hotel," Ellery said as understanding dawned. She knew exactly how much the hotel was worth. "Seriously?" For her? She was pinging all over, like ten thousand tiny airplanes were dive-bombing her skin. Like she was worth all the dollars he'd spent on the hotel. "Why, Bing? And the key, too?"

"The key—it's security."

"Like a security deposit?" She didn't get it.

"No, that's what you asked for, in a partner. Someone you could totally rely on. Someone whose word and life and everything would make you feel secure."

He'd heard that? And he'd remembered it?

"Oh, Bing." A partner? "Do you mean ... business partner?"

"Or more."

"But why?" she asked again. "Why do this for me?"

He inched toward her, a magnetism drawing her in. "I think you already have an inkling."

An inkling, maybe. "Can you brighten it from an inkling for me?" She stepped closer. "Shine a real light on it."

And he did, by taking her in his arms and placing a kiss on her lips. The kiss that sank the *Titanic*. The kiss that ignited the *Hindenburg*. The kiss that fired the starting pistol for every race her heart ever entered.

"To answer your question from earlier"—she rubbed the back of her head where she'd bonked it on Donner's neck—"yes, I'm all right."

And it seemed, perhaps, she always would be—safe and secure in the Sleigh Bells Chalet with Bing.

Epilogue

Mattie Jane

In her hotel room at the Sleigh Bells Chalet, Mattie Jane held the phone as far from her ear as possible. Rex's words were singeing it, but he was her brother. She couldn't hang up on him.

"Don't you think it's time to come back, Mattie?" Rex had made this argument before.

"I'm done with Vancouver." And with her siblings. And with having to see Jesse Parrish every time she showed up at family events. "No, I'm not *hiding out* in Wilder River. It's not like that. I'm ice climbing. I'm freelancing as an outdoor guide."

Why couldn't Rex understand that? Or anything Mattie tried to do with her life.

"Procrastination, sister." Rex was eating something on the other end of the line, so his words were muffled, as usual. "Postponing adulthood."

Yes. But so what? Not like she had a precise plan for her life that she was avoiding putting into motion. "I have a few irons in the fire. And I have gainful employment."

"Without a salary or benefits. Am I right?" Rex and his so-called maturity scoffed at her across the miles. "Come back to Vancouver."

"Say I did. You know I'll just be using the time to finish up my flight hours for my pilot's license." That'd get him.

"No!" Rex roared. "I'm serious about flattening the tires on that plane."

"Uncle York left it to me. I didn't ask him to."

"Stay out of the air, Mattie."

Just because Dad had died didn't make Rex the custodial parent. "Why do you want me to come back? Be honest."

"I just want you to get on with your life. You've been so lost since … you know."

Since Mom and Dad died. Yeah, she knew. "I'm in a healthy place."

"I don't mean your weight. Good job on that, by the way. Some guy's head is going to turn the second you set foot back in Vancouver. You'll see."

Uh, Mattie wasn't interested in turning the head of *some guy*.

Carrying an inextinguishable torch for her sister's boyfriend was sick and wrong, and she wasn't going back there. To Vancouver, to Jesse Parrish, to Naomi, or Rex, or anyone.

"The season is going really well here in Wilder River. I've met some cool people at the place I'm staying." Even though seeing that cute hotel owner fall for the horse guy had prodded awake the bear of Mattie's loneliness.

"I mean, hear me out. You might not have had gainful employment, but wasn't there something at least sort of worthwhile you were doing with your time?"

Nice. Rex *would* term her work with youth at the community garden as such. Or any of her other jobs. Which was another reason she wasn't coming back. It was the same old story. Never good enough.

"Maybe next year, Rex." When she had more of her life figured out, and when there would be fewer judgmental frowns from him and from Naomi. "How about we compromise on that?"

By then, Jesse and Naomi would probably be married. Under those circumstances, Mattie could school herself to love him—as a brother.

"I'm just concerned, Mattie. You know that."

He shouldn't be. "I'll be fine." Somehow.

A year was a good timeline. By next Christmas, she'd have her life figured out. Sensible, respectable job. Squelched crush on someone else's man. Life-plans in place.

Maybe even her pilot's license.

Yeah. Pilot. Now that was a career even Naomi and Rex couldn't sniff at. And it was one of those SMART goals—not that Mattie could recall all the words of the acronym. Something about measurable and achievable for M and A. Considering she did outright own a small plane, pilot was something she could do.

Whatever the R meant in everyone else's SMART goals acronym, it meant one thing for Mattie: respectable.

A year from now, she'd be someone her siblings, and her late parents, could be proud of.

And by then Jesse Parrish would no longer be part of all her equations.

To read the rest of Jesse & Mattie's story, check out The Holiday Hunting Lodge, *Book 3 in the Christmas House Romance Series.*

Bonus Recipe from the Griffith Family

Aunt Shauna's Hot Cocoa Mix

My husband's aunt Shauna was the consummate hostess, year-round. If you happened to stop by her house at Christmas, you'd be likely to receive a cup of hot cocoa, served with a candy cane, an orange stick, or some other embellishment. I picture this being the cocoa served at Newberg's Chocolate Shop & Hot Cocoa Haven.

1 8-quart box powdered milk
1 16-o-z. box instant chocolate powder (such as Nestle Quick)
6 oz powdered cream substitute
2 cups powdered sugar

Mix ingredients well and store in air tight jar or container. To prepare one cup of hot chocolate, use 3 tablespoons mix to 1 cup hot water. Aunt Shauna and Uncle Steve often sprinkled it on ice cream, too.

The Christmas House Romance Series

*Free full-length e-novel with baking and Christmastime romance in beautiful, snowy Massey Falls. Available exclusively to newsletter subscribers. Email jennifergriffithauthor@yahoo.com and ask for a link to this free book.

About the Author

Jennifer Griffith is the *USA Today* bestselling author of over forty novels and novellas. Two of her novels have received the Swoony Award for best secular romance novel of the year. She lives in Arizona with her husband, who is a judge and her muse. They are the parents of five children, which makes everyday life a romantic comedy. Connect with Jennifer via her website at authorjennifergriffith.com, where you can sign up for her newsletter to receive exclusive content and notices of new releases.

Made in the USA
Las Vegas, NV
20 November 2022

59636146R00080